A SHAKER OF MARGARITAS

Cougars on the Prowl

TWENTY-TWO NEW SHORT STORIES

EDITED BY L. S. FISHER

www.MozarkPress.com

Published by Mozark Press, www.Mozarkpress.com
© 2011 Linda Fisher
PO Box 1746, Sedalia, MO 65302

Cover Photo: Jan Coffman taken at the Pasta Factory, Columbia, MO.

Cover design and book layout by H. Ream.

ISBN: 978-0-9844385-3-2

DEDICATION

This anthology is dedicated to boomer women who are youthful thinkers and creative in their romantic choices.

CONTENTS

ACKNOWLEDGEMENTS

We are grateful to every author who submitted a story to *A Shaker of Margaritas: Cougars on the Prowl* regardless of whether the story was selected for this edition.

Many thanks to Jan Coffman for the photo shoot and to Pasta Factory in Columbia for making the margarita and giving us access to their beautiful, historic building.

Deepest appreciation is extended to all who proofread and assisted the editor in any way. Mozark Press would like to especially acknowledge Harold Ream for the countless hours he spent on the website and providing technical support throughout the publication process.

INTRODUCTION

When a woman becomes involved with a much younger man, she is known as a "cougar." Older women hooking up with younger men intrigue us. What is their story? Does age really matter? Is she looking for a fountain of youth and is he just arm candy? Could he be out to take advantage of her? Or did she get lucky and find the love of her life?

Authors from across the U.S. submitted fiction stories about cougars written for women who enjoy a good story without sexually explicit content or involving underage men. *A Shaker of Margaritas: Cougars on the Prowl* includes twenty-two captivating stories with boomer protagonists. Some of the stories are humorous while others are romantic—often with complications.

Boomer women were raised during an era when women didn't do what was expected, especially in relationships. Seventeen million baby boomer women are single. The older the boomer, the less chance of finding an eligible man in her age group. Expanding their "hunting" grounds to include younger men earned these women the title of cougar.

Today's women are independent and don't always need a man to support them financially. This opens up possibilities they may not have considered when they were younger.

These delightful stories will give you a glimpse into some of the nuances of cougars and cubs. What the stories tell us is that cougars aren't necessarily predatory and, instead, may be vulnerable. Like all relationships, cougars may have found the perfect mate, or realize they are mismatched. Age differences can be irrelevant, or deal breakers. Some of the cougar stories hold surprises and all relationships may not be what they seem to be.

Pour yourself a margarita, prop up your feet, and enter the world where a woman is confident enough to pursue a man regardless of how much younger he is, and smart enough to know if a cougar/cub relationship is the correct choice for her.

L. S. Fisher

Cougars on the Prowl

LOOK BACK, BUT DON'T STARE

DONNA DULY VOLKENANNT

Samara hopscotched across the parking lot, trying to dodge puddles of rain while struggling to keep her umbrella from turning inside out. At the entrance to Baum's Custom-Built Woodworking, a handsome man held open the door and waved her inside. When she brushed past him, she inhaled the scent of Aramis. Her heart skipped a beat. Aramis had been Jack's favorite cologne.

"Let me fix that."

He righted her umbrella, shook it out, and handed it back.

"Hi," he said. "I'm Van Baum."

She smiled, recognizing him right away. "Samara Graham."

"Guess our receptionist forgot to tell you to park in Visitor Parking when she set up your interview. Sorry about that."

"No problem." She brushed water off her pencil skirt and silk blouse—clothing picked out by her newlywed daughter, Emily.

Samara's black flats deemphasized her five-foot-ten height. Her wheat-colored hair, colored to mask the first signs of gray, clung to her oval face. Carefully applied make-up camouflaged tiny wrinkles across her forehead and lips.

Van had aged since they met thirty years ago, but so had she. He still dressed like a college student. His work clothes consisted of a Hawaiian shirt, baggy shorts, and safety shoes. His coffee-colored hair touched his collar. He walked with a slight limp.

Pointing at a set of stairs, he said, "This way."

They entered an office with an engraved sign: DONOVAN "VAN" BAUM, PLANT MANAGER. After pulling out a chair for her, he leaned against his polished oak desk. She glanced around his office to avoid staring at his finely toned body.

He wedged a pair of tortoiseshell bifocals on the bridge of his nose and thumbed through her resume. "Big Wolf told me you were tops."

"Big Wolf?"

"Wolfgang Baum. CEO and owner. My dad."

"When I interviewed your dad for the Business Section of *The Journal* last year, he said if I ever needed a job . . ." She sighed, "After working at the newspaper for twenty-five years, I never dreamed cutbacks would run so deep."

"I'm sorry you lost your job," he said, "but I'm glad you took Dad up on his offer."

Beats collecting unemployment, she thought, but said, "I'm grateful for the opportunity."

His smile stretched from his lips to his midnight blue eyes. "This is a great place to work. And I'm not just saying that because my dad is the owner."

She pinched the hem of her skirt, a nervous habit. "How long have you worked here?"

He took a long drink from a water bottle. "Dad hired me full-time after I graduated from college."

"When was that—last year?" She couldn't believe she was flirting with the man who had the power to hire her. She needed this job. Desperately. Mortgage payment, car note, maxed-out credit cards after paying for Emily's wedding—and here she was acting like a star-struck teenager.

A hint of crow's feet around his eyes crinkled when he winked. "More than a few years. I'm a permanent fixture."

Trying to hide her excitement, she crossed her arms across her silk blouse. "Your dad told me I'd like it here, and I couldn't believe the salary he mentioned."

"Dad's motto is 'You get what you pay for.' But we're not overly formal. Jeans are okay, but no flip-flops. Covered shoes only. 'Safety first.' That's Dad's number one rule. And everyone calls him Big Wolf."

"Big Wolf." She nodded. "Got it."

He took another sip from the clear plastic water bottle filled with tea-colored liquid. "You're more than qualified. Great job references from *The Journal*. I see you were editor of your college newspaper and high school valedictorian at Truman High."

She mumbled thanks and folded her hands to keep them from shaking.

He gave her an even gaze. "I went to Truman."

Her mouth went dry. Even though she'd kept her maiden name after she married, she doubted he recognized her.

Trying not to act overly anxious, she said, "Truman was a big school when I went there. It's even bigger now."

After she graduated from a local college, she worked part-time tutoring Truman students. Van was a freshman, rich and cute, but about to fail algebra, which he needed to pass to stay on the varsity baseball team. His mom hired Samara at twice the rate she usually charged for tutoring.

Scratching his stubbled chin, he said, "I was lucky to graduate. Algebra was a beast. Good thing I had a smart tutor."

He remembered.

When his phone rang, he glanced at caller ID. "Sorry. I need to take this."

During his call, she thought about how they'd both changed over the years. She moved away for a while after grad school, and her friends kept her up-to-date with Van's family. Later, her job at the newspaper filled in the blanks.

She knew Van's background, and rap sheet, by heart. Popular and athletic, he was an all-star first baseman. Poised for a baseball scholarship and a shot at the majors, tragedy struck. Senior year, he blew out a knee. A few weeks later, he lost his

4

mother to a heart attack. Graduation night, he wrapped his Corvette around a lamppost while driving drunk. His girlfriend ended up in a wheelchair. He broke his back. After numerous surgeries, he got hooked on pain killers and had run-ins with the law. Spent his college years on probation.

Since then he'd been married and divorced twice. No kids.

After hanging up the phone, he drained his bottle and leaned forward. His voice dropped to a whisper. "Okay if I call you Sam?"

She bit her lip. That had been Jack's pet name for her. Being called Sam would bring back painful memories, but she needed the job. She nodded.

Van extended a hand. "Welcome aboard."

Sam whispered a silent prayer. "Thanks."

He eased off his desk and handed her a hardhat and pair of safety glasses. "What kind of name is Samara?"

"Latin. My dad was a botanist. Samara means elm tree seed."

"Awesome. Kinda fits working here." Van led the way to the factory floor. "We don't use much elm, except for pallets."

In the carpenters' shop, the scent of fresh-cut lumber reminded her of summer campouts with Jack and Emily. Their last trip was two years ago.

The year she turned fifty.

The year of the fire.

Look back, but don't stare. That mantra kept away her dark thoughts.

"What about Donovan? How'd you get that name?"

"Mom's maiden name. It was cool in high school when the singer Donovan was popular. Not so much now. I prefer Van."

Sawdust hitchhiked on their shoes as they strolled to the break room. "It suits you. And yet another singer," she said. "Van Morrison."

"You like classic rock?" He plopped the clipboard down and poured two cups of coffee.

"Some." She thought about how Jack liked to sing "Brown Eyed Girl" to her.

Look back, but don't stare.

When Van said, "'Brown Eyed Girl' is my favorite," a lump formed in her throat.

After introducing her to several employees, he explained company rules. Their conversation was cut short by a shrill voice.

"Van. Return to the reception area. Stat!"

"What does she think this is—a hospital? Come on. I'll show you your desk."

Sam's desk sat next to Kimmie Gurley's, Van's most recent drop-dead-gorgeous girlfriend—a thirty-something receptionist with an annoying voice.

The women shared workspace above the showroom window. From the moment they met, Kimmie did her best to make Sam miserable and remind her of their age differences. Most days, she polished her nails, flipped through gossip magazines, or talked about how much Van liked younger women, especially her—while Sam answered the phones and took care of customers.

"So, how old are you—like sixty?" Kimmie asked the day Van mentioned he liked Sam's new hair cut.

"Not quite." Sam smiled through clenched teeth. She wanted to smack Kimmie upside the head with a magazine.

The day Sam showed up to work in a vintage dress she bought at a thrift store, Van told her how nice she looked.

After he left the office, Kimmie stuck a finger down her throat as if gagging. "Good thing he's rich. He has no taste in clothes."

Sam mumbled, "Or bimbos."

Oblivious, Kimmie said, "Do you watch TV?"

"Not much," Sam shrugged. "Why?"

"You should check out a program called *What Not to Wear*. They can help anyone, even older women like you."

Sam thought about strangling her, but decided she wouldn't look good in an orange prison jumpsuit.

Tension mounted the afternoon Van stopped by with his ever-present water bottle and started singing, "Brown Eyed Girl."

His green-eyed girlfriend said, "What's up with that? My eyes aren't brown."

Van shrugged then hummed, "You're So Vain."

Clueless, Kimmie said, "Much better."

Sam faked a cough to keep from laughing.

Except for dealing with Kimmie, working at Baum's was an answer to her prayers. Her salary almost matched the newspaper's. Benefits were generous. No long nights or out-of-town travel. And if she wasn't imagining it, Van actually flirted with her.

In no time, she knew the grades of wood. To her, each wood type had a distinct personality. Fine-grained mahogany worked well for boats. Walnut was good for gunstocks and cabinets. Maple worked best for bowling alleys. The strength of oak was perfect for desks.

Most of all, she loved the smell of cedar. Inhaling the sweet wood brought back memories of her cedar chest. The one she received as a wedding gift. The one with photographs of her family. The one destroyed in the fire.

To keep from dwelling on the past, Sam focused on talking with Baum's customers. Most of them requested her when they called, although Kimmie tried to sabotage her by "accidentally" disconnecting the phone or making shrill announcements over the intercom. And Kimmie wore flip-flops almost daily. One afternoon, Van threatened to send her home for breaking the flip-flop rule. The following morning she showed up in slingback pumps.

After taking a long drink from his water bottle, he said, "One more screw-up and you're fired. Girlfriend or not."

She replied, "Do that and I'll tell your daddy the 'iced tea' you drink all day from that bottle is actually whiskey."

Van's face turned tomato red. He stormed out and slammed the door.

After a few months, Sam was promoted to office manager, which didn't go over well with Kimmie. To keep peace, Van gave her a small raise and told her she could continue making announcements over the intercom.

When no one was around, she mumbled "Be-atch" or "Brown nose" to Sam. The name- calling didn't bother her until the day Kimmie hissed, "I heard your husband was smoking in bed, and that's what caused the fire that killed him."

Sam spun out of her chair and stormed over to Kimmie's desk, just as Van burst through the door.

"You're fired!"

"About time." Kimmie smirked at Sam then blew Van a kiss.

Sam retreated to her desk, stunned at Van's unfairness.

"Not you," he said to Sam. "Kimmie. It's over. We're over. Pack up and get out."

"What are you talking about?" Kimmie pointed a manicured nail. "She tried to attack me. Everyone saw it."

"Seriously?" Van nodded toward the customers and workers staring at them.

"You're not only cruel, you're stupid. You leaned on the intercom button. Everyone heard what you said."

She started to defend herself, but he held up a hand. "Don't even try to blackmail me. I'm getting help for my drinking problem. Leave before I have you escorted out."

When Van walked over to Sam's desk and put an arm around her, her shoulders slumped. She whispered, "Thanks for sticking up for me."

Van said, "Sorry you had to go through that. I don't know what I ever saw in her."

Sam looked him in the eyes. "Did you mean what you said?"

"Absolutely. She's fired."

Sam shook her head. "That's not what I meant. Are you serious about getting help for your drinking problem?"

Van tilted his head. "How about we talk about it tonight over dinner and drinks?"

Sam folded her arms. "Dinner, yes. No drinks. You really need help."

He cupped her elbow. "I was kidding about the drinks. How does Italian sound?"

That evening they talked for hours in the restaurant. After their main course, Van ordered dessert then leaned across the table. "Did you know I had a mad crush on you when you were my tutor?"

Sam fanned herself with her napkin to ward off a hot flash. "You're kidding. I was such a nerd."

After the waiter delivered their desserts, Van said, "No way. To me you were like a Greek Goddess. You were the nicest college student I knew and you never once called me freshman."

Sam threw her head back and laughed, throaty and playful. "I better watch out before you start calling me a cougar."

Van took a bite of tiramisu. "You're not that much older. And you look great. When I saw you run across the parking lot the day of your interview, I flashed back to listening to you talk about variables and real numbers while I was staring at your long legs."

Sam savored the sweetness of her spumoni—and Van's words. "You were such a quick learner. I couldn't figure out why you needed tutoring, but I bet you got tired of me telling you 'practice makes perfect'."

Van swiped a spoonful of her ice cream. "How could I forget? But I have a confession. Hiring you as a tutor was my idea. I watched you post an ad at the library. It was love at first sight."

"But your mom called and said you needed help."

A crooked grin lit up his face. "I flunked an algebra quiz and told Mom I needed a tutor. I gave her your number." His tone turned somber, "Mom was just so trusting."

Sam reached across the table and touched his hand. "I was sorry to hear about your mom. She was a classy lady."

"Like you." Van leaned closer. "You amaze me. After all you've been through. Yet, you're always upbeat. I drowned my sorrows in a bottle and made a mess of my life."

His tenderness caught her off guard. "Don't beat yourself up. Grief is an ugly beast. Everyone handles it differently."

"How do you handle it?"

"At first, I couldn't believe what happened. I was angry at God. Lost my faith. Blamed God. Blamed myself. I kept thinking . . . if I'd remembered to change the batteries in the smoke detector or hadn't taken that out-of-town assignment. . ."

She stopped and wiped her eyes then stared into her coffee cup while the waiter handed Van their check.

After the waiter left, she continued. "Then I rediscovered my faith. Tried to focus on the good times. Thanked God that Emily wasn't home the night of the fire. Kept busy. And I read some words that stuck with me."

Van asked, "What words?"

She paused and glanced around the restaurant, surprised to see they were the last customers. "'Look back, but don't stare.' It became my mantra."

"Look back, but don't stare. Sounds like good advice." Van stood and rubbed a knee then walked over and scooted out Sam's chair. "Wish I had your courage."

As they exited the restaurant, Sam said, "Are you kidding? Standing up for me against Kimmie took courage, especially after she threatened to blackmail you."

A light breeze rustled the rose bushes in the restaurant's garden, filling the air with the smell of roses. "And I'm going to keep my promise. I'm checking into rehab tomorrow."

"I'm proud of you," she said. "And I'll do whatever it takes to help."

He squeezed her hand. "Would you consider dating a younger man? I promise not to call you a cougar."

Sam touched his cheek. "And I promise not to call you a freshman."

Van pulled her close and kissed her on the mouth.

She lingered awhile then caught her breath. "Sorry, I'm out of practice."

"No. You're great. But if you insist, practice makes perfect."

They laughed and kissed again then strolled arm-in-arm across the parking lot, looking forward, staring straight ahead.

SHOOT FOR THE MOON

LISA RICARD CLARO

Jayne Prowse paced before her studio window and worried her lower lip with her teeth. Her assistant, Kell, made himself comfortable at Jayne's desk.

"Why are you nervous? You're a talented and successful photographer."

Jayne peered at him from beneath precision-plucked brows.

"This is America's pint-sized, cinematic darling I'm shooting. What if she won't cooperate? She's in Atlanta for just a day or two, and then she's going back to L.A. to be in a movie. There's no do-over if something goes wrong."

She resumed pacing.

"Priscilla Daybright is a six-year-old. How bad can it be?" Kell put his feet on her desk, crossed them at the ankles, and compared the buffed shine of his Armani shoes to his recent manicure. "Let's do lunch."

"You're fired," she told him.

"I'm thinking Damarino's. Shrimp bisque and crab cake special."

"I just canned you."

"I heard you." He yawned.

Jayne sighed and dropped into one of the plush visitor chairs facing her desk. She traded pacing for foot tapping.

"Are you sure?"

Kell rolled his eyes. "You need me. You might know how to photograph a possum so it looks like a purebred poodle, but you have no clue how to pair Jimmy Choos with a Dior suit. That outfit you have on, for instance. Are you really wearing that to the photo shoot with Priscilla?"

Jayne looked at her scruffy boots, faded jeans, and T-shirt that sported bold letters proclaiming: "Women Who Behave Rarely Make History."

"I look fine. Besides, she's in first grade. She won't care."

Kell set his feet on the floor and leaned forward. "You're a beautiful, fifty-year-old woman. You should dress the part." He shimmied his shoulders. "You got it, flaunt it."

That teased a laugh from Jayne. "You do enough of that for both of us, princess."

"Rainbow pride, baby," he flashed a broad smile. "Hey, what if Mr. Sexy Phone Voice is here for the photo shoot?"

"Mr. Sexy Phone Voice has a name. Chase Caldwell. And he's staying in L.A. Besides, I dress for comfort, not to impress. It's one of the reasons I love being a photographer."

"You've yet to fall for a man who makes you want to dress sexy, that's all. So, Damarino's?"

"Damarino's," Jayne agreed and stood up. She went around the side of her desk to grab her purse and cast a glance at her day planner. There was the source of her anxiety, right there in her own looping scrawl. "Priscilla Daybright headshots and candids" beamed off the page in Day-Glo pink.

Jayne bit her lip. This photo shoot would either establish her as a nationally prominent photographer or pigeonhole her as a Southeastern talent. She squared her shoulders, took a cleansing breath and turned toward Kell.

"Shrimp bisque now," she announced. "Kick-ass photography later. Let's eat."

After lunch, Kell strolled to the nearby post office and Jayne drove back to the studio to prepare for the photo shoot.

She swiped her ID card through the security reader and waited while the wrought iron gate rumbled open.

Jayne loved having her workspace in this funky, renovated factory with its sky-lit ceilings and creative, eclectic tenants. Shops and restaurants beckoned within reasonable walking distance, making convenience another draw.

Jayne strode from the parking lot and her cell buzzed as she started up the outside stairs to the third floor. She checked the caller ID: Chase Caldwell. Her heart thumped.

For weeks leading up to today's photo shoot, she and Chase shared many phone conversations reviewing details and expectations of the shoot. In the last week, the conversations became less business and more personal. Kell had dubbed Chase "Mr. Sexy Phone Voice," and he was certainly that, Jayne thought.

"Hello, this is Jayne."

"Hi, Jayne. It's Chase."

Jayne waited for the next sentence and prayed he wasn't canceling the shoot.

"Jayne, are you there?"

"Yes, sorry. Are you calling to confirm?" *Please don't cancel, please don't cancel.*

"Actually, we're at the gate."

"Are you joking?" *I did not just say that.* She gave herself a mental head slap.

"We're early. Is that a problem?"

"No, no problem at all. Please give me a minute, and I'll buzz you through."

Here? Chase Caldwell was here? If the man looked like he sounded, she'd require a shot of insulin. His voice flowed smooth as caramel candy, and she had a sweet tooth.

Jayne clicked off the phone and ran the rest of the way to her studio. She punched the gate code into the control box to allow Chase and his group entry, and tore into the bathroom to freshen up. She rummaged around the drawer but located neither toothpaste nor toothbrush, so she scrubbed her teeth with her finger and prayed not to smell like shrimp bisque. She finger-combed her hair, deemed it unruly, and twisted it into a messy bun.

Squinting into the mirror, she spied gray peeking from her temples and regretted her procrastination with coloring her hair. Had she known Chase would be here for the shoot, she would have figured the salon into her busy schedule. Maybe, she decided, he suffered farsightedness and wouldn't notice. She looked down at her frumpy attire and cursed Kell. She hated it when he was right.

Voices resonated from the hall. Jayne took a moment to send a text message to Kell asking him to get his butt back to the studio pronto, then took a deep breath and opened the door.

"Good afternoon," she said. She counted at least a dozen people, and sought out Chase.

She picked him out at the back of the group, and hid her disappointment behind a bright smile. He might sound like a sexy beast, but in person he was just a beast: big, burly, and a face no plastic surgeon would ruin his reputation trying to fix.

His smile, Jayne thought. *He has a really nice smile. Good Lord, that is a smile, isn't it?*

Jayne opened her mouth to offer a greeting, but the young hunk standing at the front of the pack stole her interest.

"Jayne?" He held out his hand and flashed a killer smile. "I'm Chase. It's great to finally meet you."

Jayne blinked. She looked from the older man to the younger, confused.

"Problem?" Chase asked.

"No." Jayne assured him, and felt a surge of relief followed by another wave of disappointment. "You don't look like your voice."

"Too buff? Too sexy?" He teased.

"Too young," she blurted, and wished she could gulp the words back down her throat. Her face heated. "I'm sorry. I expected you to be older, that's all."

"I'm thirty-two." His dark eyes crinkled at the corners. "I'm legal."

Thirty-two. You may as well be thirteen.

Jayne led the group into the studio where Chase introduced Priscilla's entourage and then the famous child.

"The munchkin is my niece, Priscilla. Priss, say hi to Jayne."

Jayne knelt to eye level with the girl, surprised to find her engaging, but shy.

"Uncle Chase says you're the boss of me for pictures today," Priscilla said. "Can you make me look like a Disney Princess? I'd like to be Belle, please."

"How about I make you look like Princess Priscilla instead? Then all the other girls will ask to look like you."

Priscilla pushed wispy bangs from her cornflower eyes and studied the ceiling for a few moments, giving it some thought before saying, "Um, no thanks. I wanna be Belle."

"Greetings, y'all!" Kell's voice boomed from the doorway, and Jayne gestured him over, glad of his arrival.

"Where's the best place to set up?" A dreadlocked man with Nordic good looks directed the question to Jayne. "I'm John. Make-up and hair."

Jayne trusted Kell to handle the group and excused herself to prepare her equipment.

Less than half an hour later, Priscilla skipped from the ladies' room wearing a red sundress and a smile. Once the photo shoot began, Jayne relaxed. Priscilla's natural star talent made her a joy to photograph. She giggled, bounced, danced, and pouted, minimal direction required. Jayne considered it her easiest ninety minutes ever spent in the studio.

"No wonder she's a top draw," Jayne told Kell after finishing the shoot.

They watched as Chase handed Priscilla over to her nanny for a return trip to the ladies' room.

"Gorgeous," Kell said.

"Yes, she is," Jayne agreed. "Here, help me with this backdrop."

"I don't mean the kid," Kell whispered. "I mean the uncle. He's to die for."

"I don't think he swings your way."

"No," Kell agreed. "But he's swinging yours."

"It looks like you got some great shots," Chase said.

"I did." Jayne nodded. "Priscilla is a natural. I guess you hear that all the time."

"Since she was a baby."

An awkward silence followed, and Jayne busied herself with her equipment. The man sent her pulses skyrocketing, and the feeling embarrassed her. Why, oh, why did he have to be so young?

"There's a nice Italian restaurant in the hotel where we're staying. Would you be interested in coming to dinner?"

Jayne's heart jumped. Was he asking her out?

"Dinner?"

"Priss loves pasta, so our whole gang is converging on the place." Chase glanced at Kell. "Please join us, too. The more the merrier. My treat. Consider it a thank you for being so terrific with Priss. You really brought out the best in her today."

Jayne's cheeks heated. She decreed herself an idiot. He didn't mean just her and him. He meant her and him and a dozen other people, including his six-year-old niece.

You're old enough to be his mother, Jayne. Get a grip.

"So, you'll join us?" Chase asked.

"Absolutely!" Gushed Kell before Jayne could respond. He nudged Jayne's shoulder and winked, then turned to Chase. "What hotel, what time? We'll be there!"

Jayne stared at the clothes in her closet. Kell was right. Casual and sloppy defined her wardrobe. Where were the spike-heeled shoes? Why no little black dress?

And what difference did it make, anyway?

She flopped on her bed and stared at the ceiling. Maybe she could beg off the dinner.

Stop feeling sorry for yourself. Who are you trying to impress, anyway? The thirty-two-year-old kid?

Yes. . .

"I am a successful, confident, fifty-year-old woman," Jayne announced to the empty room. "I don't need anyone's approval."

She stalked back to the closet and pulled a pair of black skinny jeans from a hanger, paired them with suede boots and a teal tank sweater.

"I don't feel like getting all dolled up," she said aloud. "And spiked heels hurt my bunions. So there."

When Kell arrived at her condo twenty minutes later she swung the door wide before his knuckles tapped the wood.

"Not a word from you," she pointed a finger at him. "I'm comfortable. I wear jeans because I like jeans. I wear flats because I like flats. And my hair is clipped back because I can't be bothered to fuss with it. I may even stop coloring it because it's expensive and a pain in the ass. What do you think of that?"

"Rrrowr!" Kell made his fingers into claws. "You're feisty tonight. I like it! I bet the delicious Chase Caldwell will like it, too."

"I don't care what he thinks. He's young enough to be my kid, and that's a scary thought. I kind of like the older guy. What's his name?"

"The bodyguard? Are you kidding?"

"Why not? He seems nice."

"Are you feeling okay?" Kell put his palm to Jayne's forehead. "You're dressing to impress King Kong?"

"No. That's the whole point. I'm not dressing to impress anyone. I'm dressing for myself."

"I don't know how to tell you this," Kell squeezed her shoulder as they headed for his car. "But those skinnies show off every curve you have, and the teal sweater brings out the green in your eyes. And your hair? Like you just climbed out of bed, and I mean that in a good way. You look hot. Sssssss."

"You can't talk to me like that. You're fired." Jayne laughed.

Kell grinned. "I know."

Priscilla's dinner group dwindled, beginning with Priscilla herself, who Jayne thought looked like she might drop to sleep in her pasta. The little girl blew goodnight kisses and followed her nanny. She got to the door and then ran back to hug Chase who caught her up in a big squeeze.

"Love you, munchkin."

"Love you, too." She kissed his cheek, ran back to her nanny, and waved goodnight.

"Kell and I should go, too." Jayne glanced at Kell, but he was deep in conversation with John, the dreadlocked make-up artist.

"It doesn't look like Kell is ready to call it a night," Chase observed.

"He's not," John piped up. "He's coming up to the room so I can show him how to hide under-eye bags."

Kell pushed his chair back from the table. "Wait till you see me later. I'll be ravishing."

Jayne widened her eyes at Kell in a silent plea that he ignored. Her brain scrambled now that she was alone with Chase.

"When did Priscilla first start acting and modeling?" Jayne asked. "She's a sweet child, and she's amazing in front of the camera. I don't think I took one bad shot of her today."

"She landed a part on a sitcom two years ago. It didn't go anywhere, but it got her noticed. Her real break was the role of Amy in *Seven Ways to Heaven.*"

"Is it tough on her? She's still just a baby, really."

"We keep her insulated. And she loves acting and being on set," Chase said. "If she didn't, my sister would pull her out in a heartbeat. But you saw her in action, Jayne. She comes alive for the camera."

Jayne nodded, unable to argue.

"You didn't ask, but I'd like you to know that I don't earn a penny from Priss. Her money—all of it—goes into a trust for her."

Jayne looked at Chase, startled. "I'm not judging you."

He shrugged. "A lot of people have the wrong idea. I don't want you to be one of them."

"I'm just the photographer."

"Would the photographer like another drink?"

"No thanks."

"I'm glad you came tonight," Chase said. "I've so enjoyed talking with you on the phone, but face-to-face is better."

Jayne nodded, and noted the gold flecks in his eyes. Damn, he was a good-looking man, and every bit as easy to talk to in person as over the phone.

"You sure I can't order you another drink?"

"I've already had two."

"I've only had one." He leaned forward. "I'm telling you that so you know I'm stone sober when I say the only reason I flew out for the photo shoot was to meet you. For the record, you're even more beautiful that I expected."

"Okay," Jayne said. "Maybe just one more drink."

Jayne sighed and stretched. Wakefulness arrived in slow degrees until she felt a man's warm arm slide around her and pull her close. Awareness jumped front and center.

Her eyes opened wide. She took in the hotel room, heavy curtains keeping the morning light at bay. The digital clock on the bedside table glowed eight o'clock.

She and Chase had spent hours talking and laughing last night, moving from the restaurant to the bar to poolside, and finally to his room. It was tough to feel regret with his body warming her, and it took effort to pull away.

"Hey," Chase caught her hand on her way out of bed. "Where are you going?"

"Some of us have a real job," she teased, pushing her loose hair from her face. "I have a photo shoot at eleven."

"That's three whole hours from now." He pulled her down and nuzzled her neck. His warm breath heated her skin. "Please don't leave yet."

She considered for a nanosecond.

"You win," she sighed into his kiss.

Two hours later, showered and dressed, she stood at the window overlooking the courtyard many floors below. The gardens lay lush with colorful azaleas, and for the first time in years she saw herself in the vibrant hues. Bursting with life, blooming . . .

This was a first for Jayne, spending the night with a man she barely knew. She had fantasized about him for weeks, but then she believed him to be her own age or older.

He was, she reminded herself, eighteen years her junior. What did that make her? What was that term?

Cougar, Jayne. You're a cougar.

"I'll be in town one more night." Chase stepped up behind her. "I'd like to see you again."

She smiled to herself. *A really lucky cougar.*

Jayne turned to face him and wondered what he saw looking at her now in the morning sun. Those gray hairs still peeked from her temples. Her crows' feet would be evident now, no longer softened by candle glow and moonlight.

"I'm fifty, you know," she said.

"You're beautiful," he responded. "I wanted you the minute I saw you."

Jayne laughed. "Mission accomplished."

"You laugh a lot." He slid his arms around her. "And you say what you think. You're sexy, smart, funny and slightly neurotic, and maybe a little self-conscious, but only enough to keep you from being conceited. You know who you are, Jayne, and I'm crazy about you."

"Crazy," Jayne said. "That sums it up."

"How about tonight? Dinner, dancing, a movie, a walk in the park. Whatever you want. Let's shoot for the moon."

"Are you old enough for that?" she teased. When he said nothing, she sighed. "People might stare."

Chase shrugged. "From jealousy, maybe."

She eyed the sexy stubble on his jaw and tousled hair. "Okay. I'll give you that one."

"I meant because you're so—"

She interrupted him with a quick kiss and moved toward the door, grabbing her purse on the way.

"I have to go."

"Hey, by the way, beautiful, I have a real job," Chase informed her, referring to her earlier comment. He followed her to the door and took her face in his hands. "I'm owner and CEO of the Caldwell Talent Agency with offices in L.A., New York, and Miami. My Master's of Economics is from NYU, and my MBA from Columbia. I'm smart enough to know what I want when I see it."

"Quit bragging," Jayne quipped. "I'm already hooked."

"Yeah, well, I'd like you to stay that way."

Six months later Jayne strode to her office window and peered down to the parking lot.

"No Damarino's today, Kell. I'm ditching you. Chase flew in last night. His Atlanta office opens in three weeks."

"I thought you were flying to L.A. this weekend." Kell took his feet off Jayne's desk and stood up.

"The photo shoot for the *Hollywood Rocks* cast rebooked for week after next."

"*Hollywood Rocks*. The biggest reality show on TV right now and *they* called *you*. That shoot with Miss Priss sent you skyrocketing. Everyone wants their photography done by Jayne Prowse." Kell stood beside Jayne and grinned. "You were so nervous about that job."

"Yes, I knew what was at stake. But it worked out great."

"No kidding. For one thing, you're dressing better. I should have known Chase was in town the minute I saw you this morning. You've traded your old Levi's for a pretty skirt, and you're wearing do-me heels."

"I've taken to wearing sexy shoes when I'm with Chase because at the end of the day he massages my bunions." She gave Kell a feline smile. "Bunions as a ruthless sexual come-on. Who knew? "

Jayne looked through the window again and her eyes lit up. Chase's car pulled into the parking space next to hers. He smiled and waved up at her as he climbed from the car, and her heart beat triple time. She watched him rush up the stairs and disappear into the building.

"Bunions, huh?" Kell raised a brow. "That tip could be worth millions. What other secrets are you hiding?"

"Who knows? I'm on a continuous mission of discovery," she teased, laughing as she ran off to meet her lover.

Don't Make Me Call the Flying Monkeys

L. E. Towne

D r. Laura Livingston was dressed in one of her multi-colored block print caftans, earrings the size of pocketbooks dangled from her ears. Jenny, her patient, thought they might actually be handbags, sizable enough to hold three days worth of Prozac. Jenny sat on Dr. Liv's couch, her favorite green mug steaming with lemon herbal tea was cupped in both hands.

"So, my first real face-to-face date was with someone called *God'sgift2women35*," Jenny started. "We went to a German restaurant and I listened to his presentation of scientific factoids on flashlights."

"I told you not to have high expectations," Dr. Liv said.

"God no, I'd end up with Glenn Beck's awkward cousin, so no expectations, but . . ." she trailed off. Jenny had been seeing Dr. Livingston the past eight months. Two months after a breakdown, four months after her divorce, Jenny counted her life in months and like most people, there were good ones and bad ones.

"Okay, so tell me about this guy." Dr. Liv had a unique approach and Jenny was grateful, as she could never have survived one of those serious clinicians who continually asked what do you think, Jenny? Because, honestly, Jenny didn't know what she thought.

"Yep, God's gift to women thirty-five, as if there are thirty-four more of them out there. His real name is Everett."

"Everett?"

"Yes, Everett. And he has a fetish for flashlights." Jenny sipped at her green tea. "Now this may be fascinating if you're Bill Nye, the science guy. But LED lighting is more than I really wanted to learn on a first date."

"A real Mr. Wizard, huh?"

"Oh, yes. Dick would have loved him." Jenny's ex-husband, Richard was a bit of a science geek himself. "Maybe, I'm too nice," Jenny said.

"We've talked about that," Dr. Liv answered.

"Maybe I need to be more . . . wicked." She looked at the cup in her hand. "Because my niceness forced me to listen to his lecture on light measurement and crap. He talked as if I weren't smart enough to read the side of a light bulb box. Or that I didn't have more interesting things to read."

The doctor laughed, handbags swinging back and forth, pulling her earlobes sideways. Jenny liked making her laugh. Dick had found her one-liners rather inappropriate. A year after his leaving her for a younger, paler version of herself, Jenny was just beginning to find that notion funny as well.

"Was the meal decent at least?"

"The bread was fantastic. I'll be in the gym for days, but I wasn't about to mention calories for fear of triggering another educational rant. He ordered two sides of potatoes, and a large schnitzel. Men have it so easy."

"So, he wasn't overweight," Dr. Liv said.

"No. Under height maybe, but not overweight. His profile said he was five-eight. No way that was true."

"What does your profile say?"

"I'm honest with my profile, my pictures are current. Okay, maybe I'm a bit vague about things. For instance, my profile says that I am nice, funny, and a good listener. So I try to be that."

"I would say that's pretty accurate."

"And look where it got me. His profile said he likes to learn new things. Apparently, I am not new enough to learn about. So I don't have a shiny titanium casing or I wasn't assembled in China. I'm interesting. I'm reasonably attractive."

"You are, don't let one date with one guy throw you off. It's just his opinion after all."

"Yes, yes, I know, it's not personal."

"Were you interested in him?"

"Not really, but I want someone, anyone to be interested in me. I was nice, I was funny, I told him that neutrons and short arcs sounded like interplanetary space travel and he laughed, and kept on talking about flashlights. I asked him about his life, his travels, thinking eventually he would reciprocate and ask me . . . something, anything."

"Well, you had ulterior motives, he didn't."

"I didn't have ulterior motives," Jenny huffed. "Sure, I wanted to tell him about me, the good parts anyway, who doesn't? But I wasn't about to monopolize the conversation."

"So tell me, were you really listening to his story? Or were you just waiting to jump in about you?"

"Whose side are you on?"

"I'm just trying to get you to look at this objectively—that maybe he was just being himself—being up front with you."

Jenny thought about this for a moment—that maybe she could try being a flashlight enthusiast for a few months. It would be nice to have someone to talk to, but would she talk? Or just listen?

"Being up front is what the second date is for," she answered. "The first date is for being funny and charming, and you know, pretending to be interested in flashlights."

After her session with Dr. Liv, Jenny moved through her world with a new sense of the bizarre, the new experiment into Internet dating had not gone well, but she persisted, knowing that at some point, the perfect guy would come along.

Two weeks and a few dismal first dates later, Jenny was back in Dr. Livingston's cluttered office. She was the only person she knew of who rehearsed her therapy sessions. She carefully laid out conversation points, slipping in one-liners and self-deprecating humor. Her therapist asked how she was before she even got settled on the couch. Jenny stood by the tea table, going over the good doctor's selection of herbal teas.

"I think I'll have bilious blueberry today." She plopped a tea bag into her mug. She always chose the salient green mug, with the words *wicked* on one side and *don't make me call the flying monkeys* on the other. Jenny liked the idea of being wicked.

"I don't think Yogi teas make something like bilious blueberry," Dr. Liv answered.

"Well, they should." Jenny took her steaming cup and settled onto the couch. Dr. Livingston was already curled up in the wing chair. Red leather sandals lay empty on the floor, and her feet were obscured under volumes of cotton. The caftan today was orange with bold dark slashes in alternating directions, reminding Jenny of an Arabic road sign.

"Nice shoes," Jenny said, idly wondering if she should tell Dr. Livingston about the foot fetish guy she'd met. She considered it an improvement from the last guy, from flashlights to feet. At least this one was into body parts.

"You didn't answer my question, how have you been? Still not sleeping well?"

"I've been okay. The sleep thing comes and goes."

"Anything new happening?"

"You mean with the Internet dating thing? Well, there's always something, I'm not sure it's new."

"Has Everett called?"

"Yes Everett called. I put him off. I just couldn't bear to listen to him again."

"Why weren't you honest? Just say you didn't hit it off?"

"Because he asked for my number, and I couldn't say no."

"So," Dr. Liv said, "You said yes, even though you meant no."

"Yes." Jenny sighed.

"So, anyone new?"

"A guy who wants to give me foot rubs. He's too new, meaning younger, but at least he asks questions."

"While he's rubbing your feet?"

"On the phone, I haven't gotten near him. He wanted me to take pictures of them."

"Kids today."

Janet shrugged. "Each to his own. It's just not my thing you know."

Dr. Liv sipped her tea and waited, as usual, for Jenny to launch another story.

"I had another date, someone new, but I think he's gay."

"Gay?"

"Homo-sex-shooall," Jenny drawled out the word. "I don't think he knows it though, not that I'd have a problem if he was. My sister's grad school housemate was gay. Brian was hilarious; he worked retail clothing and had great taste. Now if it had been Brian across from me, we would have had a blast. But this guy, not a clue."

"How can he not know?"

"I'm just telling you my observation. I could be totally wrong, but he seemed to have more in common with the waiter than me."

"So, tell me," Dr. Liv prompted.

"Well, it started out as coffee, during the day. I always meet during the day and only for coffee. You can't be too careful."

"Good thought."

"But he was okay you know, nice looking, not movie star looking but okay. And he asked about me, seemed to find me interesting. He seemed very lonely. Things were going well, and he asked me to dinner. I said yes. I mean, why not?"

"You do have to be cautious."

"Trust me, I could have run circles around this guy. So anyway, we get to dinner, and he says he likes movies. I ask him what kind, you know, just to have a topic in common. He starts listing all these genres. I ask what's the last movie he watched that he liked. He says a documentary."

"Oh, oh," Dr Liv said.

"Right, I mean documentaries are fine, but given my past experience with flashlight guy, I was a little worried. But I smile and ask him about it. He launches into this huge scene by scene description of . . . sheep grazing strategies."

Dr. Livingston excused herself for a moment to clean up her spilled tea. Jenny laughed watching her reaction. It *was* funny, in retrospect.

"He didn't ask you to come home and watch the sequel, did he?"

"No," Jenny answered, "we eventually went on to other things. And then this weird thing happened. The waiter, young guy, fairly attractive, excellent service all night, but all his questions were directed at my date. Which I guess is okay? Normal? I don't know. Then out of the blue, he asks my date about football—did he see the game, etc."

"Football is not really a gay come on."

"I know, and it could be just, I don't know . . . maybe the kid was obsessed with his team or something. But how would he know my date even cared about football?"

"Pretty universal guy thing."

"Right, well, I suppose if he asked about sheep migration it would be weird. Anyway, they finish talking and the kid takes the bill folder. He comes back a bit later and asks about change. My date says no, keep it. And the kid gushes about how great the tip is and shakes his hand and they launch into football talk. He even moves behind me, leaning against the back of the booth so he can get a better eye on my date."

"What does he look like?"

"The waiter?"

"No, your date."

"Kinda average—jeans, button down shirt, windbreaker. He didn't dress half as good as Brian did."

"You're stereo-typing now."

"Okay, I don't mean to, but what the hell, right? I think it was at least five minutes he stood there and talked. The kid even says, come back and see me, watch the game here, etc., etc."

"I don't know what to make of that," Dr. Liv said.

"Me, either, I was beginning to think he left his phone number and a hundred dollar bill with the check."

"So, where did you leave things?"

"We left, he walked me to my car, I gave him a quick hug and said thanks for dinner. I drove away."

"And?"

"How did you know there's an and?"

"Because there always is with you."

"Ah . . ." Jenny pauses because during this conversation she's discovered that this is not a sad failure story at all. This experience is maybe not so unique in the world of dating, but unique enough and rather entertaining. "And," she continues, "the next day, he sends me a message, something to the effect of if I wanted someone to hold me and make love to me, to give him a call."

"What did you say?"

"I didn't, for like half a day, I just didn't answer him, and then I opened the picture."

"What picture?"

"Well, before he even met me, after we'd exchanged a couple of emails, he sent me a picture. I never opened it, viruses you know? I never view pics on this site. But after our dinner, I couldn't resist."

"Oh, no."

"Oh, yes." Jenny laughed, because in the telling of it, it became harmless and funny. "It was a penis picture, in all its exaggerated perspective glory."

"And?"

"And . . . well, I printed it. And put the guy's log-in name on the back, *2sexy4U* or something, as well as the name of the dating site."

"Jenny–" Dr. Liv's tone was a spring creek thaw after a long winter.

"Yes . . . and I put it in an envelope, with football fan waiters name on it and dropped it off at the restaurant."

Dr. Livingston shook her head slightly, wrote something down on a steno pad, which was a rare thing for her to do.

"So, now how do you feel?"

"I feel great actually, and I hope they'll be very happy together."

"What a wicked thing to do."

Jenny smiled. She was wicked and funny and hopeful for the first time. Hopeful that somewhere out there was a guy who would appreciate those qualities. She lifted the salient green mug in a mock salute, "Don't make me call the flying monkeys."

THE INVISIBLE COUGAR

KATHY PAGE

Two major events happened on my fifty-fifth birthday; I started losing my invisibility, and I became a cougar. The birthday was inevitable; losing the invisibility was a mixed blessing, and at the time I had no idea what a "cougar" was.

Let me back up a little. Two years ago my husband Alvin left me for his secretary—his *much younger* secretary. While I knew he had been unfaithful in the past, it still came as a hurtful surprise. Even more hurtful was our daughter Niki's ready acceptance of the situation. Her words when he moved out were, "Well! You *have* let yourself go. Dad has a *prestigious* job and needs someone 'glam' to stand beside him." It was at that point that I started becoming invisible. Once the divorce papers were signed, I no longer existed for my ex-husband. Our daughter completely defected to her father's side and became fast friends with the new wife.

Then I started noticing that friends stopped calling. When I passed them on the street, they looked right through me. During the long walks I started taking, not one person responded to my "hello" or smile. Sales people ignored me as I wandered the aisles, and the Girl Scouts didn't come to sell cookies at my door. I assured myself several times a day that I still existed by looking at myself in the mirror. Of course, that did nothing to make me feel better. Looking back was gray listless hair, a face with no make-up, frumpy loose clothing, and a defeated look about the eyes. I realized I was slowly fading away.

On this, my fifty-fifth birthday, there were no cards in the mail and no phone calls from friends or my daughter. I was forgotten. But instead of being completely dejected I decided to treat myself to a picnic in the park. It was beautiful out, and I was ready for an outing. I had a great book, a basketful of my favorite junk food, a blanket, and all the time in the world. I could stay as long as I wanted, and no one would tell me how horrible my food choices were or that trashy novels would make my brain shrink. On the way to the park, I stopped at Starbucks and splurged for a Chocolate Caramel Frappuccino.

One person had remained "friends" with both my husband and me after the divorce. Agnes Whittington loved getting in digs about what wonderful things my ex and his lovely young wife were up to. Since she lives right across the street, she knows exactly how many visitors I don't have. It gives her great joy to tell Alvin just how pitiful I have become, all because, years ago, she heard me say she reminded me of a hyped-up orangutan. I spied her immediately at the park, but she seemed to look right through me. Either she was losing interest in torturing me, or I really was becoming invisible.

I spread my blanket under a nice shady tree, got out my book, and settled my things around me. I was about to take my first delightful taste of my Frappuccino when my world turned upside down. Literally. I looked up just in time to see a young man running backwards to catch a Frisbee. Since I was invisible, he didn't see me, and my screams just seemed to confuse him. He plowed into me, and in doing so, somersaulted me off the blanket. Chocolate Caramel drink rained down on us, and all my lovely junk food scattered everywhere.

It was at that precise moment that I became visible again. Agnes Whittington looked up to see me sprawled under a very young man who seemed to be looking lovingly in my eyes. In actuality, he was checking to see if I was still alive.

"Are you okay? Man, I didn't see you! Are you hurt? Can you hear me?"

Of course, I could hear him. His mouth was two inches away from my ear! I looked up into incredibly soft brown eyes full of concern . . . and burst out laughing! While it was good to know I was no longer invisible, I could just imagine what Agnes would have to tell everyone at the club that night. "Poor old Ellen, mowed over at the park on her birthday. Life is just so sad for her!"

My birthday plans were ruined, my body was bruised and sore, and yet it all struck me as incredibly funny. I knew I was wearing Cheez Doodles in my hair, and could feel a chocolate bar melting between this young man and myself. (Hmmm, not an unpleasant feeling at all!) No sooner had I thought this than he leaped up and started helping me into a sitting position. His arm was around me, and he kept up a concerned monologue.

"Are you sure you're okay? What can I do? Do you need a doctor? Oh, man, I spilled your drink and stepped on your Twinkies. I'll replace everything, I promise. Do you need to lie back down? I am so sorry. My name is Jeff. I'll pay for any damages. Honestly, I didn't see you."

In between giggles I said, ". . . my birthday . . . Cheez Doodles . . . Agnes is watching . . . it's okay . . . am I still invisible?"

"I think you must have hit your head. Why don't you lie down, and I'll call 911."

"No, no. I'm fine, really," I gasped as the giggles finally died away into occasional snorts of laughter. "Just let me get up and brush off some of this food. I think I'll just pack up and head home."

"Can I drive you? Or I can follow you to make sure you get home okay."

"No, no, that's quite all right. I'm fine and I don't want to put you out." Not to mention, I had no idea whether he was an axe murderer or not.

"You said it was your birthday? At least let me buy you a drink to replace the one I clobbered."

So that's how the friendship started. We walked down the block to Starbucks, found a nice table outside and formally introduced ourselves. After a few awkward moments, he burst out, "Why did you ask if you were invisible?" Trying to explain just the invisibility part of it made me sound deranged. So I told him the entire, sad story. I may have still sounded a bit deranged, but he listened quietly and when I was through, he got up and gave me a big hug. Over his shoulder, I saw Agnes looking at us from her car in the drive-thru. Great. I wonder what spin she'll put on *this* to tell Alvin and the bimbo.

Jeff told me that he was twenty-five, new in town and very lonely. I was fifty-five, newly visible and lonely. Maybe it was that extra shot of espresso, but we talked and laughed for hours.

Later he insisted on walking me home, and I can't remember when I had enjoyed a day more. It was so nice to be around such a young, vital man. I wished I could see him again but knew that wouldn't happen. Maybe that's why I felt so let down as I watched him walk away. Or maybe it had something to do with Agnes' living room curtains twitching as she spied on me.

The next morning my doorbell rang and scared me half to death. I didn't know it still worked! Cautiously I opened the door to see a huge bouquet of flowers standing there.

"Happy Birthday!" said the bouquet. Jeff's head came out around the flowers with a sheepish smile on his handsome face. "I just wanted you to feel special on your birthday, even if it is a day late."

After inviting them both in, I placed the flowers in a vase, and then couldn't think of a single, sensible thing to say. "Tea, coffee . . ." (or me?) Crap, I hadn't actually said that last, had I? Since he didn't bolt for the door, I guess a beverage was the only thing I had offered out loud.

"Um, tea is fine." My face was flushed, and I kept dropping tea bags and rattling glasses, but finally I ventured a look at Jeff. He seemed as embarrassed as I. "Look, if you want me to leave, I will. I just enjoyed our day yesterday and wanted to see if maybe we could spend more time together." If you think for a minute that I showed that young man to the door, then you have never met a lonely, once-invisible woman before.

For the next three weeks, we spent a lot of time together. I cooked for him, or he invited me out. He helped me repaint my porch and plant flowers (with Agnes watching behind her curtains), and I helped him organize his kitchen. Agnes must have lost a lot of sleep keeping track of us; there were a few nights when Jeff didn't leave until the next morning.

After one such night, I happened to be at my mailbox sorting what little mail I had when Agnes came marching down her walk. As she got closer, she stopped in her tracks. "Ellen? Is that you?" she asked hesitantly. I could understand her confusion. When I looked in the mirror, I had trouble believing it was me too. My salon lady was in heaven when I walked in two days ago and told her I wanted "the works!" My mousy hair was now a honey gold and framed my face nicely. I was still practicing with the makeup but it looked pretty good, especially since I had new clothes that complimented my post-divorce weight loss.

"Yep," I answered, "this is the new me! What do you think?"

Her eyes narrowed, "Does this have anything to do with that *boy* that's been hanging around?"

I winked and said, "I just bought him a new toothbrush to keep here."

"Well," she huffed. "Just wait . . ." She took off so fast that her housecoat started flapping.

I should have known what would happen next. Jeff and I had just finished supper that night and were on the porch with a nice glass of wine when my daughter Niki's car came screeching to a stop in the drive. She stormed out of the car and up the walk with Aaron right behind her. Aaron has been her best friend since junior high although he took a backseat for a while there when Alvin first remarried. I like Aaron; he's a steady influence on my flighty daughter and loves her madly. Aaron is also gay; more's the pity, as he would have made a great son-in-law.

"Mother, we *have* to talk!" Niki grabbed my arm.

"Aaron, this is my friend Jeff Wallace. Jeff, Aaron Jackson. There's more wine in the 'fridge!" I made quick introductions as I was hauled, none too gently, to the back sunroom.

Niki slammed the door and whirled to face me. "So, is THAT the boy toy? I CANNOT BELIEVE what you are doing! Daddy is FURIOUS! Do you know what they are calling you? A COUGAR! My mother, a COUGAR! I am too ashamed to show my face at the club!" (Niki tends to talk in capitals and exclamation points.)

"Wait, a cougar . . . what? Boy toy? I don't understand . . . and just what does your father have to do with anything?"

"Yes, a *cougar*! Bleaching your hair, toning up, fancy new clothes, showing your *legs*, new makeup . . . just so you can *catch a younger guy*! Daddy says you have *gone crazy*! It's all over town . . . my mother is a *cougar*! My life is *ruined*!" She fell onto the sofa, sobbing.

I just stood there with my mouth open trying to make sense of what she said. There was a gentle knock on the sunroom door; Aaron and Jeff walked in. Aaron headed straight for Niki and Jeff came to me. "We heard everything," Jeff said. "I'm sorry I've caused all this trouble for you." My mouth snapped shut. I went from stunned to furious in two seconds.

"Wait just a minute . . . just who have you been talking to?"

"Agnes."

"*Agnes*! So without talking to me about any of this, you just up and believe whatever that, that . . . *woman* tells you! You waltz in here after ignoring me for months, accuse me of being a . . . a . . . cougar? Of not behaving like you think I should? It doesn't matter to you that I've been lonely, that I've had my life turned upside down, that none of my friends are my friends anymore. It doesn't matter that your father married a younger woman and that you were just fine with *that*! No, all that matters are *your* feelings, *your* embarrassment. Well, you know what? I *don't care*! Jeff is my friend and that's the *only* thing that matters. If you want to sniffle around town about what an embarrassment I am—go right ahead! In the meantime, go tell your father to kiss off. He lost his right to run my life when he took up with that bimbo. Now if you will excuse me, I have more important things to deal with." I slammed out the back door. It would have been more dramatic if I hadn't walked into the trashcan, but still.

Jeff came out a few minutes later and said that Niki and Aaron had left. He tried to walk out of my life then, saying he didn't want to come between my daughter and me. Another bottle of wine and several hours later, I convinced him that what we *had* was more important than what anyone *thought*, Niki included.

Life went on, as it seems to do. Jeff was finally making some friends, but we still spent a lot of time together. I joined a women's literary group and was making some new friends of my own. I didn't hear from Niki until three months later when she called to see if she could come over to talk.

She was very subdued when she walked in. "Mother, first I want to apologize. After you raked me over the coals, I had to listen to Aaron lambast me. I have been doing a lot of thinking lately—don't laugh, I do occasionally think, you know! I never took the time to realize how hard Daddy's leaving had to have been for you. I should have talked to you about Jeff instead of listening to Agnes. I should have done a lot of things different. I'm sorry. Can you forgive me?"

A huge hug from me was her answer. "Niki, I love you and thank you for coming over to tell me this. I also know you, and it took more than Aaron and I yelling at you to change your mind. Now . . . tell me what really happened?"

"Well!" she was back on a roll. "Agnes has been spending *so* much time with Daddy telling him *everything* that is going on, that the bimbo . . . I mean *Julia* . . . Left him for the cabana boy! Agnes' husband is threatening *divorce* if she doesn't stay home and do *something* besides spy out the window! She was *so* upset that she went to the spa. The spray tanner malfunctioned and her hair dye went funky so now she looks like a *striped orangutan*!"

I couldn't help it; I was exultant! Did that make me a bad person? Probably. But it felt soooo good! "Okay, that is punishment to fit the crime, but it still doesn't explain what changed your mind."

"*Mother*! Why did you let everyone think that Jeff was your *lover*? You could have avoided all this by simply telling everyone the truth, that Jeff is gay! There *was* no *romance* between you! Aaron told me *everything*. How Jeff's mom died last year and how understanding you've been, that you listened to him and didn't judge, that you let him stay here when his landlord painted his house, that you've been such a good surrogate mother for him. And now—Aaron and Jeff are thinking about *moving in together*! I feel like I am gaining a brother-in-law . . . or something. Why didn't you set everyone straight?"

"Well," I winked. "It's not every day that a woman goes from being invisible to being a *cougar!*"

COUGARS IN CABO

KATHY HOLMES

"I'm the oldest one here," I said as I applied a generous amount of Hawaiian Tropic on my sun-starved body. Cherie never bothered to correct me that she was, in fact, older. Cherie, being proud of her French Canadian heritage, enjoyed pretending she was younger than I was whenever we were out in public together.

When people asked if we were sisters, she'd say, "Yeah, but I'm younger." Some would give her a double take and then laugh as if they were in on the joke. But, others, like men, seemed to fall for it, or maybe they wanted to fall for it. Like when we went out for drinks after work and, in the darkness, a much younger man would ignore me but make his move on Cherie. They'd dance closely together on the dance floor, make out on the sofa in the lounge until Cherie invited him to her condo. I learned a long time ago to make sure I had my own car so I could leave when it all became too uncomfortable for me.

In response to my previous age comment, Cherie nonchalantly lowered her enormous white Donna Karan sunglasses and said, "No, you're not—look at that silver-haired guy over there." *Thanks,* I thought. Just because the competition all seemed to be young, hot Hollywood celebs with long, skinny legs and flat stomachs connected by the itsiest bitsiest bikinis, and thongs in some cases, didn't mean my next best chance was with a seventy-year-old man. I was nowhere near fifty, well not unless you thought forty-seven was close enough to fifty. Cherie, on the other hand, wouldn't dream of owning up to her age, but based on the fact that she was married for the first time at eighteen and now had a thirty-eight-year-old daughter, well, you do the math.

"Okay, so I'm the fattest woman in a bikini here." If I'd known Cherie was going to whisk me away on a Mexican Riviera cruise, with two stops in Cabo, the playground for Hollywood celebs, I would have been dieting for weeks. Okay, so I was the one who had jumped aboard the ship all too willingly as the answer to my problems. Whatever the reason, I couldn't bear to assess my competition, so I stared off into the most gorgeous shade of emerald water I'd ever seen. Staring at it, studying it as if I would be quizzed about it later, I noticed it was a mix of turquoise and sea green. When I returned home, I'd redecorate my condo bedroom in that color. Oh God, what was I thinking—I couldn't bear to think about returning home to my life right now. The emptiness after Mike moved out to live with a much younger woman—or, girl, should I say—was overwhelming. He was supposed to be my second chance after my almost twenty-year marriage broke up. But scoping out the competition, I couldn't help but wonder, *Suppose Mike was my last chance?*

"As I recall from our days in southern California, the motto is, 'It doesn't matter how much money you have, it's how good you look spending it.' And I say, 'If you don't look good, it helps to have money.' "

"And we now live in San Francisco. So suppose you have neither?" I took another sip of my margarita.

"Oh, Barbara, stop with that negative self-talk. You're just wounded from that scoundrel of an ex of yours. You didn't really care about Mike—you cared more about saving face and getting back at your ex when he got that girl pregnant after refusing to have kids with you."

Ouch! But Cherie wasn't finished.

"Remember this, girlfriend. You were always the best part of that package deal. So forget about it. And Mike never lifted up your self-confidence as much as he should have. Mike and his rules—no being married before, no living more than twenty miles away from where he grew up, no this and no that. Who'd feel good enough around Mike? Find a younger, more carefree man—it'll do you a world of good." It was true, Mike and I were never the same after he discovered I'd been married before. No wonder he found a much younger woman.

And then, right on cue, the most delicious, yummy, delectable man with the darkest, curliest hair, the deepest, darkest eyes I'd ever seen, even darker than Mike's, with tanned olive skin and that smile, oh that smile, the way the eyes crinkled around the corners—strolled toward us. I began mentally primping, hoping I was sucking in my stomach enough, throwing my chest out far enough, and pasting a fun, flirty smile on my face. He strutted his stuff, moving closer and closer until I thought he might lean down and kiss me. Instead, he sauntered right past me and landed in the arms of a twenty-something. Who was I trying to fool? Like they said, "No fool like an old fool." Besides, who needed another Mike? Would he haunt me everywhere I went? What was the point of running away on a girlfriends' cruise if I was going to see him around every corner?

The feeling was a familiar one these days. I remembered when I was the young thing the young and old men were seeking. But just the other day I made a late-night trip to the grocery store and the clerk who was my age was so busy flirting with the young girls, he never noticed me. And after the girls left, he said something about "Those women who've lived a whole twenty-six years" in derision. So I thought, "Aha, we're speaking the same language." But after I smiled and made a crack of my own, he didn't even see me. I'd become invisible.

But back to Cherie and me sipping our second Cabo Wabo Margarita at the famous Cabo Wabo Cantina in, where else, but Cabo San Lucas, Mexico. Out of nowhere this dark golden tanned surf god appeared with his wet, shaggy blond surfer hair curling over one eye, surfboard under arm, accentuating the most amazing ripples, those guns, I had ever seen. And he was looking appreciatively at *me*. This time it was obvious he was interested in me, because he smiled, walked right up to me and said, "Can I buy you another?"

Lying back in my chaise with my feet propping up my thighs, I thought I'd lost it when they suddenly parted. *Talk about being obvious.* The only problem with my surf god is that he looked to be barely old enough to buy those drinks. But then, it was Mexico, so who knew if he actually was twenty-one. Cherie must have been reading my mind, "He's of age, don't worry about that." But I don't think she was reading his face when she said that, by the direction her eyes were bulging underneath her shades. Obviously, her eyes weren't the only things bulging.

Gathering all the strength I could muster to bring my thighs back together, I was relieved when my surf god extended his strong hand, gripped my hand, and pulled me up onto my feet. When was the last time a man or boy had done that? He was certainly qualified physically, but it bothered me that he was obviously so young. Did I really want to play with such a child for even an afternoon?

But then the band started playing "Does Your Mother Know" from *Mamma Mia!* and the crowd began circling us, clapping their hands, stomping their feet and whooping and hollering, "Do it! Do it! Do it!" as if they were egging us on to actually "do it" right then and there on the beach.

Being rather shy at public displays of drunken behavior, in fact, going to extreme measures to make sure I didn't appear drunk even when I'd had a few too many drinks, I also longed to let down my hair and let go, already. If I didn't do it at this age, when would I? Cherie pushed me over the top when she winked at me said, "Oh, just do it, for goodness sakes." My inner mantra was often "What would Cherie do?" in sticky situations, and I knew exactly what Cherie would do. So spurred on by all the failures I'd had in front of Cherie, I set out to prove something to her and to myself. I allowed my surf god to spin me around and I began following his suggestive dance movements. I pushed up my breasts and said, "Make room, boys," and the crowd hollered appreciatively.

And as the band played the opening chord three times, I knew it was time to get on my stage. I began singing, "Does Your Mother Know," and felt hot and teasing at the same time. At that point, it didn't matter how my voice sounded, the crowd was drowning me out. But I didn't care, I was getting into my groove. This was my moment. And at the same time when I was having the time of my life, I thought, *What took you so long?*

I spun, twirled, sashayed just like Christine Baranski did in *Mamma Mia!* I even fell to my knees and wrapped a serape around his crotch, just like she did with the towel, and the crowd went wild. But when the song ended, and the band started up a new song with a new couple in the spotlight, I intended to throw myself back onto my chaise as if it had never happened. But my young stud muffin had other ideas. Somehow feeling proprietary, he wrapped his muscular arm around me, pulled me closer, and kissed me passionately, inserting his tongue. I hadn't kissed like this in public since I was in college. And when he pulled me closer, pushing his crotch up against my middle, grinding into me, I knew that even three Cabo Wabos and a hot dance number wouldn't allow me to go any further. Even Cherie was making coughing noises, as if to cool us off.

She wasn't the only one, apparently, because before long, a bucket of ice came flying over my head. We pulled away, and I laughed nervously. Letting myself go somehow meant I had led him on, and he was misreading the entire situation. I pushed him away and ran into the Pacific Ocean to warm up after the ice bath. But he followed me. I tried splashing water at him, to keep him at bay, but a wave pulled me onto the ocean floor, and those same strong hands reached down to lift me up. It was all happening like a silent film, our bodies were talking instead of our heads. And it was time to rectify that.

"Hey, thanks for the dance and," I laughed, "rescuing me, but you don't have to stick around. I need to get back to my friend. It must be time to board the ship." I rambled on like a schoolgirl with her first crush.

"Nah, you've got plenty of time to board the ship. It doesn't sail for another couple of hours."

"Oh, how do you know? Are you cruising too?"

"Nah, I'm a surf instructor here, and cruise ships are my biggest business. It's my business to know the schedules." I was both relieved and disappointed.

Both sides of me were warring—the daring side dying to take a risk and have some fun, and the cautious side, feeling insecure and hopeless about the possibility that any man, let alone a young hunky guy, would be attracted to me. The latter one, feeling out of my element and wanting nothing more but to get back on board the safety of the ship. Who was this guy anyway? Some gigolo, no doubt. A little surfing lesson, a little sex, yep, I could see it now.

"I'm not looking for a surfing lesson," I blurted out.

He laughed, "No? I'm sure with that body you'd be a fast learner." Somehow, I doubted that. With my chest, I'd never been very good at sports, not golf, tennis, and I couldn't imagine standing up erect enough to surf without toppling over. Okay, so some women might think I was bragging, but they had no idea of the downside.

I desperately scanned the beach, hoping to signal Cherie that this would be a good time for her to intervene. But I didn't recognize anybody on the beach. I became frantic, spitting out more salt water as the next wave washed over me, trying to stay upright on my own accord without falling into the snare of my surf god. That was enough for one day—sun, sand, margaritas, and even this sexy surf god. I was starting to panic, my eyes scanning the beach for some sign of something familiar. And then I realized we had moved way beyond where Cherie and I had been sipping our drinks so innocently and happily just a few moments ago. Only now, it seemed like hours ago.

"How about going back to my place?" Just what I feared. No surfing lesson, no problem. We'll just skip to the sex part.

My look of shock and horror must have registered on my face because he laughed then and said, "No need to panic. I thought you might want to dry off, and clean up. My apartment is only a block away."

"Oh, no, no thank you. That won't be necessary. Really. I need to get back to my friend. I have a towel there, you see, and that'll be fine. Besides, I don't even know your name." Now where had that come from? I didn't want to know his name. I didn't want to be on a first name basis. Quick, I'd have to think of a fake name. No way did I want to give out my real name in Mexico. I was beginning to feel like a naïve teenager. I could see the headlines now, like an Amber Alert, only in my case, it would be a Cougar Alert: "Missing middle-aged woman in Cabo San Lucas. Last seen dancing drunk with a boy twenty years younger. Lock up your sons, mothers of Mexico, this one appears to be especially dangerous—she's on the rebound after being ditched twice for a younger woman."

And what about the pictures? I was sure I'd seen cell phone cameras going off. By now, they were probably plastered all over Facebook. At least they didn't know my name, so they couldn't tag me. I'd be known as this anonymous crazy cougar chick—I think I could live with that if I lived beyond this day. Now, where was Cherie anyway?

"Miguel," he said. Miguel, wasn't that Spanish for Mike? Oh, no, not another Mike!

Startled, I said, "What?"

"Miguel, that's my name. I'm named after my father."

"But," I stammered, "You have blond hair. You're a surf god. You look like you're from Huntington Beach."

Miguel laughed, "I am, but my father was from Mexico. He fell in love with my beautiful blonde mother when she visited here with her girlfriends on spring break."

"And how old are you, Miguel?"

"Thirty, but what does age matter when it comes to the heart? Here, I will take you back to your friend." I was relieved when he did exactly that, holding my hand, tenderly rubbing the inside of my palm as he returned me to Cherie. Affairs of the heart—yeah, right. Affair was more like it. The coconut scent of Hawaiian Tropic reached my nose before my feet reached my beach chair. And when I took in the Cherie situation, I noticed Cherie wasn't alone. Good grief—was this boy even old enough to drink? Mine suddenly looked rather mature in comparison. Cherie, Cherie, Cherie, I could count on her, now couldn't I? Or not count on her was more like it.

"Barbara, you're back. How was the swim? Or were you off doing something else?" Thanks, Cherie.

"Barbara," he cooed. "So, your name is Barbara. It's a beautiful name. Like Santa Barbara." Did he just call me a saint? Maybe it was best I let him think so. That way he wouldn't be dragging me off to his apartment any time soon.

"Wait one moment," he said, and I sat down on my chaise and applied more sunscreen on my body before Miguel offered to do that because then I knew I'd be hopeless once his hands were rubbing my body. At the same time, I tried not to hear the slurping noises next to me—slurping when this boy kissed Cherie's neck, lips, arms, hands. I was afraid what he'd kiss next. Or what I'd want Miguel to do to me next.

Miguel returned with a tray of fish tacos, and until now, I hadn't realized I was famished. "Bless you, Miguel, I'm starved." Had I really said, "Bless you?" Who did I think I was, Saint Barbara?

He grinned, looking happy that he had pleased me. Beyond his god-like status, he was thoughtful and kind, and we spent the rest of the afternoon talking and laughing about crazy tourists. But when it was time to return to the ship, he handed me his business card. "I sometimes spend summers in Santa Cruz," he said, "So give me your number, and I'll give you a call."

Oh, what the heck? What harm would it do? Besides, he'd never call. But what a fabulous souvenir from my trip to Mexico.

On the bus ride back to the ship, I thought about the age difference and how I felt about it. I was flattered, no doubt, but a cougar, I was not. Cherie, I was not. As for Cherie, well, Cherie was a real-live cougar. I was only a cougar in Cabo. And a reluctant one at that. But one fabulous cougar afternoon was enough to bounce back and regain my self-esteem, and I'd be forever grateful for that. And I now knew that anything was possible. I found myself sitting taller and grinning bigger. Cougar. Huh! Me? Imagine that.

THE SCARLET LETTER "C"

DEBBIE PARKER

I am cougar hear me roar. Why is it that when men date younger women they get a pat on the back and a wink? However, when women date younger men they get a capital "C" Velcroed onto their shirt like Hester Prynne? I think of myself as being in my prime rather than as a predator huntress on the prowl for my next prey.

Matthew and I met at the Java Hut at the university where we both work. I usually drink coffee at home, but one day between classes I decided a strong Joe would lift my spirits after a run-in with an unpleasant coworker.

I walked in, fumbling with my umbrella and book bags, and juggling all my paraphernalia, when I heard a decidedly masculine voice say, "Hi. You look as though you could use a cup of coffee. Is it still raining?" I looked up into his azure blue eyes, saw his winning smile, and that he was taller than my five foot ten. The deal was sealed on my being physically attracted.

I tried to think of a witty repartee, but words eluded me. All I could do was mouth, "Yes. Coffee, please." I felt like a perfect idiot until my friend reminded me that nobody is perfect. I wasn't sure if she meant I wasn't a *perfect idiot* or just not perfect. Sometimes it is better not to give things too much thought.

When I went back for a snickerdoodle cookie, he added, "I hope it lets up soon. I told my retired neighbor I would help her with her yard work this afternoon."

Did I actually hear him say he was going to help an elderly neighbor, or was I hallucinating? It's hard to say with the imaginary harp playing in my mind.

Once I found out he worked on Tuesdays and Thursdays, I started going between classes to have a latte, because they take more time to make than just a cup of coffee. Luckily, I was prepared the next time I went into the coffee shop. I made sure my hair and makeup were just so. It wasn't raining and I left one of my bags in the office.

"How is your neighbor? Were you able to get some of her yard work done for her?" I asked.

"How sweet of you to remember," he replied and asked my name for the order. I really didn't see a reason for him to ask because I was the only person in the place at the time. *This is hopeful*, I thought to myself.

I continued to go in for another month and we exchanged small talk, but not phone numbers. As my coffee consumption increased and my wallet got lighter, I knew one of us had to make the first move.

On the very day I had built up the courage to ask Matt to go on a date, he asked me out. "Kate, I really enjoy talking to you, and I'd like to get to know you better. We can't have a real conversation while I'm working. Would you like to go out for dinner or a drink some time?"

"That would be nice," I replied. It would be more than nice. It is hard to show interest without looking desperate. *Nice, couldn't you show a **little** more interest?* I thought to myself. I knew better than to tell my friend and have her remind me again that nobody is perfect. I'm aware of that already.

When my thirteen-year-old daughter, Jennifer, found out I was going on my first date since my divorce five years ago, she told me she had some advice. I was concerned about what her words would be and more importantly how she knew that much about dating. I exhaled a huge sigh of relief when Jennifer said with a serious face, "It's okay to hold hands, but don't let him kiss you. Ashley knows all about this kind of thing and she told me." I thanked her for the advice and made a mental note not to let her have any sleepovers at Ashley's house.

My daughter also helped me pick out the *right* outfit. I wanted one that didn't scream *Mom*, yet I didn't want to look like a coed with a skirt so short it barely covered my assets. I finally decided on the proverbial little black dress. It's classy but not frumpy—the way I like to think of myself. I did, however, wear four-inch stilettos with the intention of sitting as much as possible. I planned to park close to the door, even if it meant driving around the block ten times.

As I waited for Matthew to arrive at Tellers, I contemplated what I should drink. It was easy when my ex-husband and I dated because he always drank beer and I had Earl Grey tea.

My friends told me that the drink you order conveys a lot of information about your personality. Ever helpful, they told me not to order a drink with an umbrella because it looked too frou-frou and superficial. If I ordered a Jack and tonic on the rocks, I sounded too knowledgeable. Since I'm neither, I took the easy route and asked the server what she recommended. I had my plan in place when my date arrived.

In walked my Adonis, but after I put on my glasses, I saw it was actually someone meeting his model-like partner who was as gorgeous as he was. Shortly thereafter, Matt walked in wearing a tasteful navy jacket and khaki pants. He cleaned up nicely, but I still can't get used to the unshaven look. What's up with these guys who don't shave? Are they afraid of razors or just too busy to use one?

"I hope I haven't kept you waiting too long. My mother called, and I needed to wish her a happy birthday."

"That was thoughtful of you," I replied thinking he's sensitive and kind. Check box one—handsome. Check box two—considerate. Check number three—employed, even if it is part-time because he is a graduate student. Is it safe to assume that he likes kids too? Nah, that would be too good.

"How old is she?"

When I heard the answer, I lost my appetite. That's when I decided to make the drink a double. After I ordered my martini and Matt his old-fashioned, we tried to get to know each other.

"So, Kate, I'm dying to know more about you. I've always found you easy to talk with. Your insights and ideas make me think about you long after you've left. Also, you have the kind of beauty that is very attractive because you're pretty, but you don't act as though you know it."

Pinch me. I'm dreaming. No, on second thought, let me sleep because I like this dream. When I thought about my interests, I sounded like a middle-aged single woman and tried to think of a way I could put a spin on my hobbies. After all, I did teach advertising.

I didn't feel I could say that I like to read, cook, and make greeting cards, so instead I said, "I like to dabble in the arts. What about you?"

"I enjoy fantasy football, the WWE and walking with my dog, but I don't have a lot of free time because of my genetics research project."

I fantasize about football players, I thought to myself. "Joe Montana was always one of my favorite quarterbacks."

"Doesn't his son play for Notre Dame?" Matt responded.

"It could be. I think that my father used to watch Joe play pro." Of course, I watched him on TV with my father. I needed to be more careful about age references.

Let's try again, I thought. "I've been a member of the WWF for years now."

"You're so funny! One of the things I've always found attractive about you is your sense of humor. I like World Wrestling Entertainment but of course the World Wildlife Federation does wonderful work."

Great, now my hearing is going. At least, we have dogs in common unless he said frogs or something similar.

After a few dates, I thought that it was safe to accept an invitation to a family gathering at his parent's home.

"Kate, is that you? I haven't seen you since college," I heard shortly after entering the house.

"Oh, I see you've met my Uncle John," Matt said taking my hand.

"Yes, we've actually met before," I answered sheepishly.

"Kate, Let me introduce you to my wife."

"Bambi, this is an *old* friend."

I thought that John stressed the adjective a little *too* much.

Matt, always one to help defuse a situation, offered to take Bambi to get a drink and meet some other people.

"What are you doing dating my nephew? He's at least ten years younger than you!"

"Well, what about you? You're old enough to be Bambi's father!"

"That's different. She's a girl."

"She looks more like a woman to me, barely legal, but still fully a woman," I responded.

John said he had other people to talk with and excused himself. It only got worse when I met his mother who was wearing a Chanel suit similar to mine. It's embarrassing enough to be seen in the same outfit, but when it is your boyfriend's mother—it is beyond humiliating. I immediately went home and added it to the ever-growing bag of clothing for the Salvation Army.

A couple of months later, we decided to take the relation-ship to the next level. Kimberly was going to spend the week-end at her father's house, so we planned a weekend trip to Mexico. This would give me a chance to wear some of the new clothes I'd been buying just for Matt. I felt safer wearing them in a country known for its less formal attire.

As we were walking down the street holding hands, a couple about my age my age said in Spanish, "*El is joven, pero ella no es*" and laughed. My Spanish was good enough to know that they said that he was young, but I wasn't.

I didn't know whether it was my short skirt and tight top that made me look *older* or if I was just trying to fool myself into thinking I looked good.

Anyway, between clothes that make me feel matronly and clothes that my friends call *mutton dressed as lamb*, I'm running out of things to wear.

I'm not sure where this relationship is going, if anywhere, but I do know that I'm happy even if I am wearing a big scarlet letter "C" on my chest.

School Days

Cathy C. Hall

"How can I help you ladies?"

The tall salesman stuck out his hand. "I'm Jack," he added. "And you are?"

Carol shook his hand, but she wasn't ready to give her name to a complete stranger.

"Looking for a car," she replied.

"D'uh." Her daughter, Lizzie, rolled her eyes.

Carol Patterson's insides clenched nervously as she stood next to a taupe pre-owned sedan, her hand fiddling with its side mirror. This was the first time she'd ever been at a car dealership alone. Or rather, been car shopping without Tom at her side. But she couldn't put it off any longer. Her jeep had seen better days when Tom was still alive. Now, two years later, she thought she should just shoot the old car and put it out of its misery.

"So, are you looking at this car for you? Or your sister?" Jack the Salesman smiled. He rested his arm against the hood of the car and leaned in towards them.

Carol wanted to roll *her* eyes at that remark, but instead she blushed. Her fourteen-year-old rolled her eyes instead, and sent her mother the "ewwww" look at the same time. Kids were great at multi-tasking like that.

"It's for me," Carol replied, willing her face to return to its normal color. There was just something so attractive about this man. Tall, dark, handsome, Jack the Salesman fit the bill in the classic looks department. It had been a while since Carol had responded to a man in that way. She swallowed hard thinking of "that way." She couldn't even bring herself to think the word *sexual*.

"It's a great car," he said, "especially for the price." He glanced at the sticker.

"I'm not sure," said Carol. "I was hoping to find something for less than that."

Jack the Salesman's smile stayed put. His dimples were awfully cute. "I don't think we could come down much from $12,000. That's a sweet deal. But maybe I could sweeten it up a little more. For you."

Carol's stomach did that flippy thing. She wasn't sure if it was sticker shock at how low he was willing to go, or the way his blue eyes locked onto her green ones and wouldn't let go.

Jack the Salesman was flirting with her. Big time. She flushed uncomfortably.

"Miss Cherry?" The salesman cocked his head. "It's Miss Cherry, isn't it?"

"No one's called me that . . . well, it's been a long time." Carol smiled.

"Wow," he said. "This is unbelievable! Miss Cherry, *here*!"

Carol didn't think it was *that* unbelievable. She'd lived in this area for the last twenty years or more. But in all that time, she had to admit she'd never come across any of her former students.

Lizzie came around from the back of the car. Apparently, Jack the Salesman had finally managed to grab her attention.

"You were in my mom's class?" asked Lizzie.

"Oh, yeah, Miss Cherry's class." He smiled broadly. "Everybody wanted to be in your mom's class. I mean, Miss Cherry was, um . . ."

Carol blushed even brighter red this time. Though why she should, she didn't know. She'd been twenty-six when she came to Granger High School as a brand-new teacher, with her Farrah Fawcett hairstyle, perky boobs, and suede boots. She knew the boys in her class drooled over her. Though sometimes, they drooled because they fell asleep. Still, she bet she'd starred in quite a few freshman fantasies.

She returned Jack the Salesman's smile. "Young and single," she said, to help him out.

"Yeah," he said, obviously grateful. "I was in your last algebra class. You left that year."

Carol thumbed through her memory, trying to place this much more mature face. She hadn't thought of those teenagers once, not since she'd left the hallowed, hormone-crazed halls of GHS. Three years of ninth grade classes had done her in. Homework just couldn't compete with Homecoming.

"I got married that summer," she said. "And we moved . . ." That had been the excuse at the time. Carol would have moved to the moon to get out of that classroom!

"So, how's your husband?" he asked.

"Deceased," said Carol. She wasn't trying to be funny. She just didn't want any more questions about Tom.

"Oh," said Jack. "I'm sorry. Really."

Carol busied herself, reading the sticker very carefully. "Thanks," she mumbled.

"Mom? Can we go? I'm going to Madison's tonight, remember?"

Of course, she remembered. She wasn't over-the-hill yet.

"Let me give you my card," said Jack, reaching into his pocket. "Or hold on a sec. Why don't we get together this evening? I have a proposition for you."

Carol cleared her throat. A proposition? Goodness, this guy worked fast.

"Come on," he said. "You'll like it."

Carol wasn't so sure she *would* like it. But she *did* like Jack the Former Student's sexy smile and the way his eyes were twinkling mischievously.

"Okay," she said. And she gave him her number.

"Mother," said Lizzie, the minute they got back in their own car, "I *cannot* believe you gave that guy your number. He's like fifty years younger than you."

"First of all, I'm not even fifty years old myself. I'm still forty-nine, thank you very much." Carol pulled out of the lot. "Which would make Jack . . . thirty-four. Maybe thirty-five. That's not that big of a deal."

Though Carol's hands were sweating now, thinking of the age difference. Fifteen years? Was she crazy?

"Maybe if you live in Hollywood." Her daughter slumped in her seat.

"Oh, so now I'm a . . . what is it, a leopard? No, wait! A cheetah!"

"Ugh. It's *cougar*, Mom."

"Are you sure?" she asked. "Because I really like the sound of cheetah." Carol laughed, teasing her daughter.

Her laughter was long gone by the time she left for the restaurant. It had been replaced with the urge to scream. Or hide. She walked into the restaurant, anyway, figuring at the very least that she'd get a decent meal.

Jack waved to her from the bar. He held an appletini in his other hand. "Want one?"

"I think I'll pass," said Carol. She needed her wits about her. And she had no idea what was in that glass. When did martinis become green?

"It's kinda funny, me sitting here with Miss Cherry, drinking." Jack flashed his killer smile.

Off to an awkward start, she thought, forcing a smile back to him. "Why don't you call me Carol?"

They ordered food and Carol manipulated the conversation to restaurants in the area. That seemed like a safe topic. All through dinner, they discussed where to find the best burrito, or the perfect pizza, or the juiciest steak. But somehow, from Jack, simple words took on extremely suggestive meanings. Juicy, tender, delicious . . . Carol was just considering a cold shower when Jack got to the point.

"About my proposition," he said, raising his eyebrows in a roguish attitude.

"Mmmm . . . tell me about it," she said, lulled into a chocolate torte stupor. She met his eyes and the adjective "smoldering" popped into her mind.

"I guess you remember that I wasn't the best algebra student," he said.

For a change, Jack was the one squirming uncomfortably. Honestly, she still couldn't remember him. But then again, the majority of her students hadn't exactly been math majors.

She batted her eyelashes, trying to appear interested. Even though she'd rather not revisit those 'rithmetic days.

"So I'll just say it," he said. "I never graduated from high school."

Oh, the poor thing, thought Carol. He's sitting over there, feeling inadequate around this older, educated woman. All that bravado was just a mask for his insecurity. He darn near broke Carol's heart.

"That's not . . . it's nothing, really," she said, jumping in to soothe his ego. "I mean, look at you. You've got a great job! You're doing really well."

"I know," he said.

That wasn't what Carol had expected.

"But I want to get my GED. So I can go to college. I think I could go further at the dealership if I had a degree. Maybe a few business classes."

Good for him! She admired his pluck—and his courage. It wouldn't be easy, going back to school at his age.

"I think that's a great idea," she said. "I'm sure you can do it!"

"I thought I could do it, too. But I've kinda hit a roadblock. The same old roadblock I hit when I was kid, back in your class."

Carol cringed when he said "kid." Why did he have to say kid? She waited to hear what the roadblock would be.

"Um, it's the math," he said, giving her Lizzie's patented "d'uh" look.

"Oh! The math!" Was Carol an idiot? Of *course* it was the math.

"You probably remember how I used to mess up numbers? Get 'em turned around all the time?"

Carol's brain squeezed out a memory at last. A lanky kid with a pimply face, standing at the board with his book in hand. He'd copied an equation with 87y in it. Except it had been *78y*. She could see it plain as day. That had been the moment she'd realized why the boy kept flunking tests. He was dyslexic. Not hugely dyslexic. But enough to cause mix-ups.

"You're PJ," she said.

"Yeah, well, everybody on the basketball team called me PJ. I guess there were a lot of us in your class."

Carol pasted on a fake smile. The basketball players had been a handful that year. Her head started to throb, remembering *that* nightmare.

"So, um, Jack," she said. "You still have problems with that?" She hated to say "dyslexia" because she didn't know if he'd ever been diagnosed.

"Yeah," he shrugged. "But if I'm careful, it's all good. It's just that I'm having trouble with some of the concepts, too. I mean, it's been a long time. I guess I don't need to tell *you* that."

Suddenly, she didn't feel nearly as fine as she had a few minutes before. In fact, she was sure indigestion was in her immediate future. Thirty-five-ish Generation XYZ men like Jack probably didn't have to worry about old-age diseases like indigestion.

"I'm sure it'll come back to you." She sipped her water.

"I was thinking you could help me with it? The math?" He leaned in to her. "Sort of tutor me. It'd be just like old times." His top lip curled, fetchingly.

Carol's chocolate torte sat like a brick in her stomach. And speaking of stomachs, she was sick and tired of holding hers in. She exhaled and shook her head.

"I don't think so, PJ," she said. "Once was enough."

She stood up and handed him a twenty. "For my half of the dinner." It wouldn't cover the tip. Not that he'd know.

"You don't . . . that's not necessary . . ." he stammered. She noticed that he slipped the twenty in his pocket.

"I still want to sell you that car!" Jack the Salesman was back at work.

Carol fingered her keys and thought about that taupe car. The one with the $21,000 sticker price. He'd thought it read *$12,000!*

She almost laughed out loud, but smothered a giggle just in time.

"No, thanks," she said, throwing her scarf around her neck.

She'd had enough of school days with Jack. But maybe she'd take a second look at some of the guys in her office. After all, this cheetah could still run!

SPECIAL ON MELONS

JENNIFER DICAMILLO

Beth pulled into the far reaches of the grocery store parking lot. She considered the longer walk her exercise for the day. Climbing out, she locked her car and started toward the building with a quick step when her attention was drawn to a stock boy joyriding on a cart. The parking lot had a downhill slant, which made the cart pick up speed quickly.

The stunt was dangerous, and it only took a second for the fun of it to lose its sparkle. A car turned into the otherwise quiet lot, a little quicker than was reasonable, and the cart couldn't be stopped fast enough. Tires screeched. Beth yelled a warning, too late.

With a sickening thud, the cart crumpled under the fender of the blue Buick, and the boy slid, all too neatly, underneath the entire mess. Beth fumbled for her cell phone in her pocket as she ran toward the accident. Simultaneously, she prayed the kid would be all right.

By the time she reached the actual scene, the driver was out of the car, bending under the far side of the car. Beth's heartbeat rapped a hard and fast tattoo, and she wondered if she'd have a heart attack at the sight of a dead boy. She feared the worst.

The distance across the parking lot seemed ten times farther than it normally would have. And Beth admitted to herself, she was too old for this sort of excitement.

"You have reached 9-1-1. If this is not an actual emergency, please hang up and dial 555-4736. If it is a true emergency, hold on and your call will be answered in the order it was received."

Beth swore under breath, which was now coming in gasped spurts. She reached the Buick.

The driver, a young mother with three toddlers in the back seat was bending over, repeating, "Oh, God. Oh, God. I'm so sorry."

Beth cleared the front of the car and was relieved to find no expanding puddle of blood. Before she managed to see the victim, the operator came online.

"This is 9-1-1. What can I do for you?"

"For me?" Beth stuttered, trying to catch her breath. "There's been an accident," she huffed.

"What is your location?"

"DiBiase's Grocery Store Parking Lot." Beth looked wildly around, trying to remember the street names at the closest intersection. Normally, she was quite bright, and very together. Extremely lucid and capable for a woman of sixty. At the moment, though, she felt as if she'd lost her brain, and her vocal chords were on their way out the door, too.

The kid under the car said to the driver, "Calm down lady. I'm all right . . . I think."

Relief flooded Beth and the driver, both.

"I just need help getting untangled here."

Tony DiBiase, the grocery store owner, appeared, helped the boy climb out from under the car, and jostled the bent-up cart free from the fender while Beth stuttered into her phone a little more.

"Hey, don't call an ambulance. I don't need to go to the hospital." The stock boy looked more embarrassed than hurt. "I'd refuse it if it showed up."

"Oh, God. Please don't say he needs to go to the hospital." The driver panicked. "I don't see any blood."

There were bound to be bruises, and Beth knew the boy should be checked for worse, but Mr. DiBiase held out his hand for her phone and she gladly gave over the responsibility in favor of asking the boy her own questions.

"You sure you're okay? How's your head? Did you hit the pavement?"

"Nah. I just slid under the car, kinda neat-like. I really am okay. No harm, no foul. The cart was like a roll cage." He offered a small smile to the driver, and lowered his voice. "If you don't tell my boss I was riding the cart, I won't tell anyone you ran me over."

"Oh, God. I did, didn't I?" The actuality of the accident sunk in to the driver's brain. She began to shake all over.

The kid patted her back. "Come on. Relax. Look, no blood. No bones sticking out. Let's pretend this never happened."

"Yeah . . . yes." The driver nodded, backing toward her car door.

The next thing Beth knew, DiBiase handed her the phone, the call finished, and announced, "Why don't you all come inside and we'll see what we need to do here."

His gaze of concern went over the victim first, the driver next, and finally Beth. It lingered so long, she felt her blood pressure rise. It was distinctly more personal than necessary.

He's probably thinking I'm too old to jog across the parking lot without having a heart attack. Thinking I'm the one that may need the ambulance.

She spared him a glance and had to hold back the gasp that struck her solar plexus. Mr. DiBiase was one of the most handsome men Beth had ever laid eyes on.

Of course, she'd heard stories about him, and that's why she finally came to shop in his store. But she never suspected he'd have such an effect on her at first sight.

It wasn't love, of course. But lust, definitely. And considering, at her age, she'd nearly forgotten what reaction a body could have to real sex appeal.

He was only about five foot ten but had a definite Italian machismo going on. *He must be around forty*, she guessed.

From her experience, Italians were either fair or dark. Tony DiBiase had the best of both, as far as she could see—a full head of jet-black hair, graying at the temples, and alert blue eyes, an aquiline nose, and perfect lips above a strong jaw line.

Beth fumbled, putting her phone in her jacket pocket, her gaze locked with DiBiase's. "I, uh, saw the accident. So, I think I'm the only witness."

It seemed unnecessary to state, but her tongue worked of its own accord, with a need to establish some sort of sane conversation. Sanity seemed to have left her. How could she feel so stunned by a man's looks? His presence? His energy?

"Why don't you come inside and we'll talk about what you saw?"

The kid shook his head. "There ain't nothing to talk about. I'm okay. We should all just go about our business. I've got pickles to put on the shelves."

"Let me at least pay for the cart damage," the driver insisted.

"That won't be necessary," Tony assured her with a calming smile, glancing over her shoulder at the children who were making noise in the car. "Why don't you bring the kids in and we'll—"

"Actually, if he's fine, I'd rather go home. I'm a little shaken up, don't want to shop now."

Beth worried her bottom lip, not wanting the woman to leave the scene of the accident. What if the boy was really injured internally?

He dragged the mutilated cart around the building, disappearing. The driver reached in her car, retrieved a piece of paper from her purse and wrote down her contact information.

The whole thing played out in slow motion to Beth, but only took a few moments. Before she knew it, the driver was gone and Tony DiBiase had her by the elbow, helping her toward his market.

Inside, he steered her toward his private office and offered her a beverage. She selected a fruit juice, and sat down with him sitting next to her in the second chair in front of his desk.

"My name is Tony. DiBiase. I own this store."

"I . . . I figured as much." Beth took a sip of the Strawberry Kiwi drink, and screwed the top back on the bottle.

Mr. DiBiase picked up the phone, called the kid's mom and asked her to come pick him up. "He says he's fine, and he doesn't appear bruised, nor is he bleeding, but I think you should check him out yourself. I will, of course, cover any medical bills incurred. But he really seems fine."

His voice had a smoothness to it, an assurance that things would be all right. And he used the same tone on the overhead speaker when he called the boy to his office, and told him to get ready for his mother to pick him up.

The kid argued his healthy state, but Tony didn't take him at his word. Beth liked the way the man took charge, and did the right thing by his employee, showing more concern than the victim wanted.

The entire situation seemed out of her control. Why she sat limply, watching everything happen without responding much, she couldn't guess, except that she was totally taken by Tony DiBiase. Or maybe she was in shock.

After all, it was scary to think back and replay the incident. She'd been horrified at the thought of getting to the car and finding the boy dead or bleeding.

But, after the boy's mother arrived and took him away, promising to take him to a doctor to get checked out, promising to bring the bill to Mr. DiBiase, Beth finally perked up, her worry assuaged.

It didn't matter that Tony DiBiase was probably twenty years her junior. His touch on her elbow and forearm assured her that things would be all right. His tone, his intense gaze studying her face, gave her the impetus to pull herself together.

"Mr. DiBiase," she finally managed.

He quickly insisted, "Tony."

"Tony." Beth licked her lips. While she'd planned on saying something firm, like "I really must go." Or "I think I'll save my shopping for another day." Her insides rolled over like mush and jelly, and she felt decidedly feminine. Not that she didn't always feel like a woman, but she felt girlish, a state she hadn't felt in a long, long time.

"And you are?" His smile kindly invited her to share her information.

"Beth. Beth Winston."

He glanced at her hands. She wondered if he was checking for a wedding ring. Of course, she had hers on still. Her husband had died seven years earlier, but Beth hadn't even considered taking the ring off. She'd worn it since she was nineteen. It was a part of her.

His disappointment was palpable. She watched him swallow heavily.

His knee bumped hers. He reached for her free hand, the one without the ring, the one not holding the drink. His fingers were warm, like the smoky gaze he sent her.

And Beth realized he didn't care if she was married or not, or that she was twenty years his senior. He was attracted to her in the same instantaneous way she was to him. Or maybe his attraction had grown over the few moments they'd shared together.

The moment should have been awkward. She should have moved her knee away from his, or withdrawn her hand abruptly, but Beth suddenly felt empowered to be bold.

Without any more hesitation, she said softly, "I must confess, I find you extremely attractive . . . for a grocery store man." Her lips turned upwards. Why she'd added the little jibe, she wasn't sure. Perhaps to alleviate the seriousness of her announcement.

"And you, Mrs. Winston," He leaned a little closer, "are, perhaps, the sexiest woman I have met in a long time."

Sexiest? Beth's insides sizzled and curled and climbed up her throat. She had to cough to clear it.

Boy, was she glad she'd had her hair done the day before, dyed auburn, cut in a modern layered style, and done her make-up before coming shopping.

"Well, I wasn't expecting you to say that." She grinned, but looked away. What was she doing? Flirting? She hadn't flirted in a hundred years!

"I have to admit," Tony confided, "I don't usually find myself attracted to customers."

She should have felt let down instantly, but her mind recoiled with *Technically, I've never shopped in your store.* In fact, she'd only come because all the women in the garden club insisted she do so.

"The man shamelessly enjoys his job."

"He turns the produce section into a steamer."

"I go just to look at the man. He's sexy, that's all there is to it."

"He can talk about canned goods and make a woman drool."

"He's running a sex shop; oh, it may look like a grocery store, but more men in this town have had good sex after their wives shopped at DiBiase's than . . . well . . . you just *have* to go, Beth."

And here she was, like the entire garden club, swooning while being told he doesn't *go* for customers. She was too old for him, and she knew it. She needed to thank him for the beverage and take her leave.

"Good policy," she said, pulling her fingers from his hold, simultaneously setting the bottle on his desk while standing up. She expected him to stand up, too.

But he sat there, looking up at her with something akin to confusion. She resisted the urge to touch his cheek and plant a kiss on his lips.

"I just wanted you to know." His voice quiet, he finally stood up.

While he didn't touch her, she felt as if he'd climbed upward, using her for a ladder. Every part of her body titillated at his closeness. Her head tilted backward, as he was taller than she was.

He was too close, barely a half inch between their bodies, a definite encroachment on her space. She'd be deaf, dumb and blind not to get his interest. While it baffled her a bit, she felt more empowered than she'd ever felt with a man, and she liked the fact that he was encouraging her without stepping over any lines of propriety.

If there was to be anything between them, it was her call. Totally up to her.

The tension built while she considered the possibilities, her mind running rampant with sensual probabilities. Taking a chance, she let her fingers slide forward, touching his. She figured she'd pretend it was accidental if he . . . but he took the initiative to slip his fingertips up to the inside of her wrist, then press his thumb into her palm, pulling her hand against his hip, cupping it there.

He was having trouble swallowing. She could see that as he searched her face for something, she wasn't sure what.

Tipping forward on her toes, she pressed her lips to his, and closed her eyes, waiting for rejection. Not because anything about him signaled he would deny her, but she expected it because she was so much older than he was, and a stranger to boot.

Tony's lips softened, parting gently. His free hand slid around her, lightly caressing, drawing her close enough for the fronts of their bodies to touch. The scent of his cologne, spicy and musky-sexy overwhelmed her.

The kiss was everything romantic and promising she'd ever dreamed of, yet nothing more. Thankfully, he didn't slip her the tongue, or crudely grab her ass, or grind himself against her in a vulgar way.

The thoughts, unwelcome and unexpected, reminded her of her husband. Too often, he'd ruined a good moment with crassness. Of course, he'd had a license to take his privileges as he chose. Thirty years of that, and she fully expected it of men.

So, Tony DiBiase was a surprise, a completely pleasant surprise. As she took her lips from his, and opened her eyes, she half expected him to say something crude. Or anything. But he didn't. He held his tongue. He watched her, waiting for her to make the next move.

Their fingers were still entwined. His other hand lightly had the small of her back.

Huskily, she said, "I came for a melon. I heard they were on sale."

Not missing a beat, he smiled. "And they are ripe and sweet."

"Maybe I'll take two."

"We have home delivery. Did you know?"

"No. I had no idea." Frowning, she added, "The stock boy didn't look old enough to drive."

"I do the deliveries."

Beth's eyebrows shot up. Did he have a special delivery thing on the side with several of his customers?

No. What was it he'd said? He didn't find himself attracted to customers?

Leaning his forehead against hers, he whispered, "I see you think too much."

"Somebody should be thinking here." The retort came quickly, before she could think about it. And that brought her to a need to confess. "I'm older than I look."

"Over twenty-one is all I care."

"You would like a twenty-two year old?" Of course, he would!

He growled. "I like older women. Women old enough to . . ."

"To what?" She drew back, challenging him.

"Old enough to appreciate a relationship without games."

Beth licked her lips. A relationship? Boy, was he getting ahead of himself.

"Whoever said anything about a relationship?"

Tony backed up a foot or so, putting his hands on his hips, frowning, chewing on the inside of his cheek. It took him a minute to come to terms with her little quip.

"Look. I haven't been this attracted to a woman in a long time. Not at first sight. You took me by surprise. But I can assure you, I intend to pursue you, unless you tell me you can't stand the sight of me."

"Even if I'm married?" She held up her ring finger.

Tony spared it a glance, and she could see he was struggling with it, but he shook his head. "You kissed me."

It was true. Even if she'd been married, that kiss screamed of want and need. It told on her . . . that she was emotionally unattached.

What could she say to that? How could she deny the thrill of excitement that sliced through her when he announced his intentions of pursuing a relationship with her?

Straightening her back, she informed him, "I'm probably twenty years older than you."

"Then why are we wasting time talking?"

She had no good answer, so she stepped forward, into his arms.

COUGAR CAPER

C.A.NEILSON

The cool thing about being a cougar is never knowing how a day is going to begin or end. Cat toys with this idea as she reads an article on dual realities her friend Taylor posted on Facebook at 7 a.m. Today, for instance, seems completely predictable—having tea while reading this stimulating article and checking up with online friends, then slipping into mostly mundane chores all laced with the anticipation of meeting her friend CK in Tigertown for a bit of shopping and dinner. A simple reality, lacking in chaos or duality, yet completely open to whatever unexpected surprises might pop up along the way.

So Cat's not surprised when, later that afternoon, she gets to her favorite resale shop, New Beginnings, and immediately finds the perfect vintage jacket for CK's son's fiancée. She didn't even have to look really; she pretty much just walked right over to the rack and found it waiting. Aqua velvet, black jet buttons, a beaded collar, tiny tucks at the waist giving just a tad of flair, and on sale to boot! CK's subsequent arrival confirms the selection, and the shopping part of their outing concludes in a snap.

"Now what?" CK pulls out a psychedelic purple faux leather wallet and waits for the clerk to total her purchase.

"Dinner, I guess." Cat fingers a pair of heart-shaped earrings on a display stand. "We could go to Uprise."

CK runs her hands over the velvet jacket. "This is just so perfect . . . anyway, I love that place but I'm bored with their menu."

The woman at the register keys in the amount then gives CK the total. "You could go to the Vault," she interjects, "they're having a BXR listener appreciation party. Free food and giveaways."

"As in BXR the radio station?" Cat asks.

"As in," says the clerk as she bags up the jacket.

"I love that station." Cat turns to CK, grinning. ". . . at the Vault . . . where secrets are kept. A perfect place for cougars like us to prowl."

"And free food," replies CK. "I say we go for it."

"Indeed."

Since it's only a few blocks and there's only a mildly bitter chill to the night, they decide to walk. The District street lamps cast long shadows across their path, making them look like characters in some spy noir movie from the 40s. While they walk, Cat warms her fingers by texting her friend Taylor. "The Vault's his favorite mixed-drink bar in Tigertown. Can't pass up the chance to rub it in."

CK tightens the muffler around her throat. "I can't wait to see it for myself . . . especially after all the hype from you guys."

"You'll be pleased, I'm sure." Cat stares down at the reply from Taylor, just popping up on the screen. She laughs and reads it out loud. "So jealous . . . maybe you should bring me a Manhattan . . . have fun, cougars."

CK glides through the revolving door into the bar, her predatory instincts kicking into place. "Cougars, my ass. He should be so lucky."

"Touché on that."

A marble staircase leads them down to their destination where a voluptuous woman in black leather and silk greets them. "I'm Leslie. Thanks for listening to BXR and welcome to the Vault." She points to a silver box. "Please do sign up for our door prizes. You do have to be here to win though."

Cat eyes her youth then returns a confident smile. "We're not going anywhere."

The two women head to the bar, where Cat waves at Aaron. The bartender, decked in his usual yellow polka-dot bow tie, shakes a slick silver mixer, ice knocking against its sides like dice on wood. She and CK grab two stools and Cat makes the introductions.

"So you're the expert mixologist?" CK bats her eyelashes at the attractive younger man.

"So I'm told," Aaron hands her a drink menu, "but you can decide for yourself. I'll be back in a jiff to get your order."

"Well, what do you think?" Cat asks, soaking in the ambiance—the cast of red patterning the dimly lit room, the risqué period photos offering the smallest suggestion of indiscretion, leather seating, and the sound of a piano breathing itself into the air.

CK looks up from the menu and joins Cat's perusal. "It's fabulous. I can see why you're so taken with it."

"Taylor's more taken with it, but then, it suits his style completely. I'm just a bystander who gets to look in the window from time to time."

CK loosens her muffler and settles into the back of her chair. "I think it suits you. Maybe it's just that the style is new to you and not completely comfortable."

Cat considers, her eyes reflecting the sultry environment. "I hope you're right."

Aaron's return focuses their attention on the matter at hand. "What'll it be, ladies?"

Cat doesn't need to think about this one. "I'm starting with Jamesons neat and the free food."

"Way too many choices, but I think I'll go with the Fancy Pants . . . and I'm all about the free food too."

"I had that one last time," Cat sighs. "It's fabulous."

"Help yourself to the food, ladies, while I serve these up for you."

Sliding off her chair, Cat notices a familiar face entering the bar. She nudges CK. "There's that guy we met at Beks a while back," she says, referring to their weekly happy hour date at Fulton's premiere dining locale. "Remember, the one who's a counselor at the prison."

CK's gaze follows hers to the door, toward a man with sleek glasses, wavy hair, and a full sensual mouth. "Hey, you're right."

They move in the direction of the food, taking them directly across his path. CK puts out her best smile and says "hi" which causes him to draw back, apparently startled.

She whispers to Cat, "That was weird."

"Yeah, almost like he didn't know us or want us to know him. Bizarre, huh?"

Needless to say, they're moderately shocked when, a few minutes later, the same guy appears at the bar and asks if he can sit next to them.

CK never misses a beat. "Please do." She gives him her best cougar smile even though the guy is probably their age and not in any respect cougar material. He's not bad looking though, so worth the effort.

He's almost stealth-like as he moves onto the chair, then orders a gin cocktail without even looking at the drink menu, obviously a Vault regular. Small talk becomes the order of the moment, not amounting to much of anything until finally CK gives him a long hard stare that she, being a lawyer, normally reserves for moments in court. "You don't remember us at all, do you?"

At this point it's his turn to stare, though his doesn't measure up in its intensity. He takes his time studying them both, however. "Well, you do look familiar, but I'm not really sure from where."

CK and Cat exchange looks before bursting into near-raucous laughter. No wonder he'd acted so strange. Probably not used to hot mature women hitting on him in dark 20s-era bars.

Finally Cat decides to give the guy a break. "We met you at Beks . . . at the bar."

Slow recognition dawns on him like a twenty-watt bulb. "That's right! I thought maybe you'd seen me here, but now I remember. Of course!"

Being the self-assured women they are, Cat and CK ignore the fact that they obviously failed to make a memorable and lasting impression on this guy, writing it off to the fact that he's more than likely an idiot with a really bad memory. No harm, no foul.

Still, unimpressed with his skills at recall, Cat turns to enjoying her Jamesons and nachos, leaving CK to question the guy about things he'd told her on their previous meeting, during which Cat also enjoyed other things while CK did the talking.

After a lengthy session of what's going on with regard to this and that, he sat back in his chair, astounded. "I can't believe you remember all that! After only one conversation and months ago at that!"

CK shrugs off the compliment. "I'm a lawyer. It's my job to remember things."

"Uh, there's one thing I don't think we remember though," Cat interjects, looking at CK for confirmation. "That would be your name."

"Oh, yes, that's right. I'm terrible with names."

He's not immediately forthcoming with this information. "So what are your names?"

Cat has no qualms about giving up this irrelevant piece of info. "Today I'm Cat, but ask me tomorrow and it might be something different. My friend here is CK."

"I would have figured you for a Rita."

Cat looks slightly offended. "Rita? That's weird. I don't think I look like a Rita at all."

"At least it's got a couple of the right letters," he says. "What's with the changing your name thing?"

"Let's just say I don't always plan it, but sometimes it just happens."

CK snorts. "And sometimes you do plan it . . . Cate, Catelyn, Cathlynn, Cathy, etc., etc."

"Okay, yes, sometimes I plan it. So what, pray tell, is your name?"

This time he gives up the ghost. "Rick."

"As in Casablanca," Cat muses, "and here we sit in a dark bar where secrets are kept. Nice."

CK chimes in with curiosity as she swirls the remaining contents of her Fancy Pants. "Do you have any secrets, Rick?"

Rick doesn't miss a beat this time, as if the revelation of secrets pales in comparison to giving up his name. "Oh, tons. For one, I'm a spy."

Alcohol kicking in by this time, it takes several moment of intense laughter from both women before one of them finally manages to say, "You're kidding."

"No really. I spied on the Czechs in Europe."

"Say something in Czech then," CK says.

"*Ahoj krasna zena.*"

Cat bursts into another round of laughter. "That's pretty impressive." CK turns to her friend. "So why are you laughing?"

"Because he's bull-shitting us."

"You think? I don't speak Czech but it sounds pretty authentic to me."

"Oh come on." She leans in toward Rick. "You are bull-shitting us, aren't you?"

Rick responds with complete seriousness. "No."

Cat keeps her eyes focused on his as she takes a lady-like swig of her Jamesons. "So you really are a Czech spy?"

"No, I'm an American spying on the Czechs."

"Oh, pardon my faux-pas."

"Actually I sometimes use PAX as my code name."

"How appropriate." Cat shakes her head with disbelief at the lengths he's carrying the charade. The only other explanation being that he truly believes his story, which would be frightening.

While CK continues to prod Rick about the spy thing, Cat picks up her phone and sends Taylor another text, eagerly sharing this latest and thoroughly unexpected discovery. His quick reply makes its appearance a moment later, "Serious? I think I met that dude last time I was up there. Weird."

Cat reports this information to CK and Rick then immediately hoping to add to his jealously sends Taylor a photo of the *Catcher in the Rye* she's just ordered. "Can't get much better than Jim Beam, limoncello, and the Vault," she captions it.

"Taunting wench," he responds.

Rick, who's been staring intently at CK's ankle for some time, finally asks about her purple-patterned tattoo. "It's a Celtic knot."

"So what is that exactly?"

CK sighs and begins a rout response. "Lots of Trinity symbolism . . . Spirit, Mind, Body . . .Father, Son, Holy Ghost . . . Mother, Father, Child . . . Creator, Destroyer, Sustainer . . ."

"Interesting . . ." He looks at Cat who's still checking for texts. "Do you have one?"

She lays her phone on the bar, a relatively safe distance from her water. "What, a tattoo? Hell, no. That would require being touched, which is a no-no for me."

Rick picks up his gin and swirls it. "You don't like to be touched? What's that about?"

"Probably something to do with watching my parents getting murdered in front of my eyes when I was a kid, which ultimately led to my current stint as a vigilante serial killer."

"Is that true?"

"She's lying through her teeth," CK answers.

"No more than he with the Czech spy thing."

"I think I'll find out." Rick slides off his chair and moves toward Cat with predatory intent. She starts screaming even before he touches her, causing Aaron to do a double take in her direction.

"She's okay," CK tells Aaron, then questions her judgment when Rick actually does touch her, causing an escalation in the volume of her discomfort.

He immediately hurries back to his seat. "Okay, I'm not going to do that again."

"Thank God." CK glares at her friend then changes the subject from murderous rage to foot positions on barstool chairs. "I saw this really interesting thing yesterday about how you can tell whether someone you meet in a bar is interested in you or not. If their feet are facing toward you, they are; if they're facing away from you, they're not; and if they're straight on, they're ambivalent."

Cat, completely recovered from her cacophonic outburst, glances down at her own legs. "So what if they're crossed?"

"I think that's ambivalent, too. Makes sense . . . kind of like closing yourself off to the other person . . ." Realizing the more sexual implications of this statement, she blushes slightly but luckily it's covered by the room's hint of red.

Cat hasn't picked up on the remark and it's anyone's guess whether Rick did. "I guess I'm ambivalent then . . . that stands to reason, since I'm pretty ambivalent about men in general."

"Why's that?" Rick wants to know.

"Difficult divorce."

"Recent?"

"Sort of but not so much." She nudges CK. "Ask my attorney."

Rick turns his attention deliberately back to CK. "Oh, so you represented her?"

"No, I did not." CK shoots Cat her own murderous glare. "She wanted me to represent the lying asshole, so I told them both to shove it. I'm just her plain old regular attorney now."

"That's her," drones Cat, "my plain old regular attorney who knows all my secrets except the one about being touched . . . who refused me in my hour of need."

"I did not refuse you and you know it . . . at least when it really counted."

Their eyes meet with voiceless understanding. "I know," Cat says.

"So is that really his name?" Rick asks. "Lying asshole?"

Cat looks at CK with a lighter gaze. "Oh, we should tell his name, shouldn't we? In case they ever meet. After all, they do live in the same city."

"Absolutely." CK reveals the name of the lying asshole.

"Don't know him . . . will try not to."

CK lifts her glass for Cat to photograph the dregs of her drink for Taylor. "That would be wise."

Rick watches Cat as she types into the phone. "Who *does* she keep writing?"

"Her friend Taylor. This is his favorite bar, and she's taunting him mercilessly about our cocktails."

"He wouldn't happen to be that guy who works at Beks, would he? The one who wears the hats?"

"Yeah, that's him. He looks like Johnny Depp. Do you know him?"

"I've seen him there, and I don't think he looks like Johnny Depp."

Cat stops texting and faces Rick with a stern expression. "Really? Seriously?"

Rick stands firm. "No, I think he looks like a young Marlon Brando . . . like when he was in *Streetcar Named Desire*. He wore a hat too."

Cat ponders this for a moment. "Yeah, okay, I can see that. No earrings or purple hair though."

"Well they weren't exactly in vogue back then."

"Taylor would be horrified at you using 'in vogue' to describe his hair."

"Good thing he's not here then, and please don't text him that information. I might have to kill you." Rick downs the last of his gin cocktail then sets the glass on the bar. "Well ladies, it's been lovely, but I've got to be at work tomorrow morning, so I must bid you both a fond farewell. Thanks for an enchanting evening."

"Hey, aren't you going to give CK your number? I mean, I think you guys might be soul mates . . . I haven't been completely oblivious to your conversations about left-wing politics and peace affiliations . . . and while she may not have been a spy, CK is the reincarnation of Marie Antoinette."

"And she still has her neck," Rick notes. "Sure, CK, I'd love to give you my number, if you'll be so kind as to accept it. With your cakes and my undercover skills, I'm sure we'll go far together."

CK retrieves her purple-fabric encased phone. "I'll put you in here right now. Oh, let me take your picture too." She makes him face her full-on and snaps the shot then keys his number into her iPhone. "Excellent. You are now at my disposal."

Rick takes her hand and places a light gentlemanly kiss in her palm then moves in Cat's direction. "You're not going to touch me again, are you?"

"Never." He points his finger within an inch of her then waves it up and down, child-like.

"Cute," she says.

"*Bonsoir*, ladies." Rick makes a slight bow, retrieves his coat from the chair, and retreats.

CK and Cat watch him go in silence. "One for the road?" CK asks Cat.

"Why not?" She notices Rick's muffler on the floor. "Damn, he must have dropped the stupid thing. Order us one while I see if I can catch him."

Quickly navigating the stairs and the revolving doors of the Vault, Cat spots Rick leaning against the wall, smoking a cigarette, another spy noir image which this time brings a slight smile to her face. Next to him is an attractive Middle-Eastern-looking man in a black turtleneck and thick tweed jacket, also smoking. She holds out the scarf. "I think you dropped this."

Rick looks at her as if he's never seen her before. "Not mine." Dismissive, he turns back to his conversation.

Cat shakes her head, disbelieving that the evening seems to be ending the way it began. She traces her steps back into the bar, quickly relating the exchange to CK. "I could have sworn I saw him wear this earlier . . . and he acted like he'd never even seen me before. Maybe he really is a spy . . ."

"Stranger things . . ." CK replies.

Outside of the Vault, Rick, alone now, opens his phone. He pulls up a message box and addresses a note to Taylor then writes, "Thanks for heads-up on the hot cougars. Perfect cover. No one suspected a thing."

Inside the Vault, Cat and CK sigh over the lingering final taste of their cocktails. "These really are excellent, Aaron." CK hands him several bills with their check. "You deserve this nice fat tip."

"My pleasure, ladies. I trust you had an enjoyable evening with your friend there. Hope to see you in here again soon."

"You can be sure of that, my friend. It was delightful and incredibly revealing." Cat pulls the cherry out of her *catcher*, savors the fruit then holds up the stem. "Speaking of Celtic knots, I used to be able to tie one."

"Really?" says CK. "So prove it."

Cat pops the stem into her mouth, works on it a few moments then produces the finished product. "Voila!"

"Okay, I'm impressed." CK pulls out her phone and takes a photo. "Power, intellect, and love . . . another Trinity. Tonight went really well, don't you think?" She slides Rick's empty gin glass toward Cat, who slips it off the bar into an all-too-receptive purse.

"I'll say. You got his eye scan with the photo, and now we have his DNA. By morning we'll have a sketch of his contact based on my sighting."

CK's seductive laugh flows around them. "Your little sweetheart at Beks played into it perfectly. Just like you said he would."

Cat's smile reflects immense satisfaction. "Do I know men or what?"

"You do indeed. So, now I think we should treat ourselves."

Cat scans the room, her eyes pausing on a couple of muscular young men not far away. "Those two have been watching us all night. Shall we go for it?"

CK follows her eyes then shakes her head. "I was thinking ice cream."

"Ah . . . yum. Let's do it."

Giving Aaron a quick wave, they grab their bags and start for the door. "Hang on a sec. I just want to finish this up." She pulls out her phone and starts to text.

The woman from the resale shop opens her incessantly chiming phone. A photo of Cat's knotted cherry stem pops up on the screen. Smiling with satisfaction, she reads the message, "Mission accomplished. Cougars rule."

Kentucky Cougars – An Endangered Species

Kim Lehnhoff

I'd never considered dating someone younger before. I mean, I figure the "adult activities" would probably be a bit more plentiful, and energetic, than with men my age . . . but I just could not imagine the quality and subject matter of the pillow talk.

What would we have in common, besides lust?

I was relatively new in town and hadn't joined any social organizations yet. And my new female co-workers were all happily married, so they were not a good source of potential dates. Loneliness and the Internet gave me an opportunity to test my theories about dating a younger man. I checked out some online personals, and even posted an ad that was funny, a bit naughty, and upbeat. A recent photo was displayed prominently—I had no desire to engage in false advertising.

Each evening after work, I'd come home and turn on my laptop while I ate dinner, alone. I was getting a lot of responses to my ad. Some of the emails I got were downright creepy, others, simply boring. I responded to each and every one of them. To the rejects, I'd post that I had already met someone, and I wished them success in their search.

I began an email correspondence with Ricky420. His name made me giggle—my name is Lucy. I couldn't help but wonder if I was going to "have some 'splainin' to do!"

He was a divorced dad of three young children, was gainfully employed, and could construct a complete sentence.

Fifteen years my junior, I was surprised that we had things in common; he and I shared an interest in camping, reading historical novels, and we both loved attending live theater. Ricky seemed to be an affable fellow, and I was only mildly leery about giving him my telephone number.

Our initial telephone conversation went well. He got points for calling when he said he would—I was pleased to hear that he used good grammar and diction on the phone, and didn't mumble. I really liked his laugh and was pleased that we didn't have awkward silences during our chat. We talked on the phone a few more times before Ricky asked me out to dinner.

Being a semi-veteran of online dating, I knew to be cautious. I agreed to meet Ricky at a Mexican restaurant.

That Friday evening, I was especially careful about how I dressed. I did not want to appear the least bit matronly, or remind him of a kindly schoolteacher from his past.

Ricky's photo did not do him justice . . . he was gorgeous. Tall, with dark brown, wavy hair and a smile so engaging it took my breath away—just for a second. I hoped my appearance didn't disappoint him. If he had any doubts about me, he hid it well, and we fell into easy conversation while we waited for our food.

"Ricky, I need to ask you something. You're a good-looking man and could have your pick of just about any woman around. Have you always dated older women?"

Ricky smiled an awkward smile. "I've dated women my age, or a bit younger. I *do* get hit on quite a bit, but I'm tired of their games, I guess. They either want me for eye candy, or as a daddy to their children. Many are too promiscuous, and want a 'friend with benefits' which doesn't interest me at all. I want a relationship, not just a one-night stand. I can't stand barflies and don't want to hang out in smoky bars and then listen to my date puke in my bathroom."

He paused, and I nodded encouragement for him to continue.

"Some women seemed more interested in my checking account balance than in me. One girl trotted me out in front of her friends to show me off. What she didn't know is that some of her girlfriends slipped me phone numbers when she wasn't looking. I never took them up on their offers—I figured they were all cut from the same bolt of cloth."

Oh goodness, isn't he a confident fellow? God's gift to women right here in front of me, I do declare! I took a long drink of water, mostly to hide the smirk that had crept upon my face. "Come on, Ricky, do you really think all women your age—wait, all women behave that way? That attitude doesn't speak well for us of the weaker sex, does it?" I could hardly wait for *this* answer! Our waitress approached to refill our glasses. Her cleavage was as big as the great outdoors, and she made a point of bending over a bit when she filled Ricky's glass. He'd have to be blind not to see the girl's "assets." I watched with bemused interest as he quickly gave her perfunctory thanks. *He's either one smooth operator, or he means what he says. I'll have to keep my eye on him.*

"After my divorce, I discovered the rules of dating had changed from when I was in high school. I started dating older women after I talked with some of my mom's friends about the quality of women I was meeting. I realized older women were confident without being arrogant, and knew exactly what they wanted out of life—and weren't afraid to ask for it." He took a drink of water and continued. "They like what they see in the mirror each day and don't have the simpering insecurity of younger women. They don't primp and preen or solicit validation for how pretty they are. Older women don't play games with men's hearts and minds—a quality I find attractive."

When it appeared that he was done telling me his take on women, I watched as he took a healthy swig of his margarita. I guess he needed to wet his whistle after his analysis of the fairer sex. I also took a drink of my margarita, needing to feel the coolness of the drink as well as the fire of the alcohol slide down my esophagus. I thought I'd heard everything a man could tell me, but I was wrong. I don't know if, at that moment, I wanted to touch him, or make him an appointment for a therapist. Talk about ambivalent!

Again, Ricky smiled. "Okay, Lucy, it's your turn. Why are you interested in dating a younger man?"

"Well, men my age seem so set in their ways. They've lost their sense of wonder—they're jaded, I suppose. They're lazy, or have no energy, or have decades of experience mistreating their former partners—and assume I'll tolerate the same behavior. I won't, by the way. And to be frank, middle-aged men lack imagination in the bedroom, and think if they're satisfied, then I must be, too. They have no idea that sexual attraction starts long before you get into bed, and sexual desire can begin with words and kind gestures." Now, it was my turn to smile; I'm sure my face showed my concerns. "Hearing you talk, I wonder why I hadn't considered a younger man before now, if all younger men think as you do. It seems that I could have the pick of the litter." I wanted him to know that I was not going to be as easy a conquest as he might hope.

Ricky had quite an appetite—and by appetite, I mean he ate with such gusto that I feared he would inhale the plate right off the table. Apparently, table manners weren't a priority when he was growing up. Immediately after I had that thought, I felt old, and judgmental—after all, he *had* said he was famished, and I know he worked hard all day, in his job as head groundskeeper for a Lexington country club.

Our conversation during dinner, and a shared pitcher of margaritas, helped me forget my misgivings about his dinner etiquette. After all, I wasn't his mother, so why should I care if he shoveled food in as if there were no tomorrow? All I had to do was gaze into his piercing blue eyes, and I could forget about that spot of sour cream and pico de gallo that dribbled down his chin.

Ricky had planned to make the two-hour drive home after dinner, but after those margaritas, I wasn't sure he should be driving. Menopause changed how my body metabolized alcohol—I could drink a couple of drinks without any ill effect, so I offered to drive us to my place for coffee. Ricky asked if I could stop at his friend's house so he could pay him for a favor.

So we took a short detour into a subdivision on the seedier side of town.

I sat in the car while Ricky walked up to his friend's front door. He looked just as good from the back as from the front. He must have spent considerable time in the gym; his body was lean and toned. Yummy. I fiddled with the car radio, looking for a station that would provide romantic background music for our drive back to my place.

It was not my habit to take men I had just met to my house. I could hear my daughter's voice in my head, telling me "be careful, there are 'creepers' out there." But there was something about Ricky that made me feel simultaneously aroused and maternal, and not in some sick incestuous way. I could see myself taking care of him, holding him—whoa, I was getting ahead of myself.

Ricky smiled his thousand-watt smile as he slid into the passenger seat. He leaned over and gave me a tentative kiss on the lips. "Thanks for making the detour," he said, as he ran his fingers through the back of my shoulder-length hair. He sat up and sighed, a wicked little grin on his face. My hand, trembling just a little, turned the key in the ignition and put the car in gear.

I pulled into my driveway and smiled at Ricky. He kissed me again, and reached across me to unlock the driver's door. "Just sit still. I'll come around and open your door properly," Ricky said, smiling. He loped over to my side of the car quickly, and in one motion, opened the door, took my hand in his, and pulled me to my feet. He pulled me close to him, and his breath tickled my ear. It felt so good to be held like that. Kissing my cheek, he stood back a step and took my hand, and we walked toward my front door. Feeling a bit giddy, I wondered if old Mrs. Godfrey was looking out her picture window at the shameful behavior occurring across the street.

I told Ricky to relax on the sofa and went into the kitchen to start the coffee. Instead, he followed me, and sat at the kitchen table. While I was busy getting mugs out of the cabinet, I heard him unwrapping something plastic, and turned around to see what he was doing.

There, on my kitchen table, sat a baggie of pot, and a packet of rolling papers! I hadn't seen that stuff since my college days. He grinned sheepishly and started to roll a joint, and casually asked, "Want to join me? It'll help us both relax."

That half pitcher of "liquid courage" failed me at that moment. I was shocked and confused. I imagined what my children would say—what my *son* would say, my son the K-9 officer for our local police force. How would I get the smell of pot off my table? Bleach? Windex? Would Rusty, the German shepherd, be able to smell the pot?

Ricky noticed the horrified look on my face. "Oops, sorry. Thought you'd be cool with it. I mean, didn't you grow up during the 60s?" He laughed and put the dope in his jacket pocket.

He pulled me onto his lap, kissed my neck and whispered apologies and sweet nothings in my ear. Purring in my ear, he held me close and told me how he'd like to take me to bed and grab onto my hair and have me call him "Daddy."

I jumped up like a woman on fire. "I don't know how girls your age act, but you've got a lot to learn about grown women, young man! I don't even know you, you presumptuous twit!" I was livid. "First of all, I had a 'Daddy,' and he would never, ever treat anyone like that. Second, you have a lot of nerve! You asked me to drive you to your drug dealer, for God's sake—then you want me to jump in bed with you and call you 'Daddy'? Do you have any idea who you're talking to? Get out!" I shouted, "And don't ever call me again."

I hurriedly looked up the number for a taxi, and we sat in stony silence until the cabby honked from the driveway.

After he left, I was shaking in shame and disbelief. I used four different solvents on that table. It had never looked so clean.

I swore off dating younger men in that moment. From now on, any future dates would be with men my age who shopped for Budweiser, Grecian Formula and Viagra, not cannabis.

Or maybe I'd just give up dating altogether and get a dog for companionship.

THE ILLUSION

TRACY HAUFF

Splat. A sigh of annoyance escaped from Malinda's classic red lips, but she held her tongue. She wasn't going to re-hash petty disagreements tonight. In their first year of dating, she and Jared had argued about Copenhagen daily. She had never been exposed to chewing tobacco before and found it disgusting, but Jared assured her that cowboys chew. They pack their lower lip with tobacco before riding into the arena, but before entering a dining establishment, they do the polite thing—get rid of the brown saliva-laden mass by spitting it out. If a container isn't available, the parking lot will do. She would never get used to it.

"Good evening," the hostess gushed. "I have your table ready for you." Malinda had requested a corner table to hide them from curious eyes. She wasn't sure how Jared was going to react to her news, but that wasn't the only reason she wanted seclusion. Their appearance always turned heads, and she was weary of the unwanted attention. At forty-eight, she presented an attractive, chic, successful business woman while Jared had the rugged good looks and lean physique of a thirty-two-year-old professional cowboy. No one ever assumed they were mother and son, or sister and brother, partly because Jared was very affectionate, but also because they portrayed exactly what they were: an older woman with a younger man.

"Take off your hat, please," Malinda reminded Jared. He obliged by placing it brim side up on the chair beside him. He ran his fingers through his hair and gave his head a slight shake, a signature move that used to electrify Malinda. His thick dark waves fell obediently into place, framing his tan chiseled face and resting on his starched collar.

The waiter appeared. "Would you like to start with a cocktail or some wine?" he asked.

"I need a few minutes to look at the wine list," Malinda responded.

"Certainly. If I can assist you with your selection, please let me know."

"I have my heart set on lobster so I'll be having white. I think . . ."

"I'll take a Bud," Jared interrupted. "And a T-bone. Rare."

The waiter flashed an accommodating smile. "Very well, sir. I will bring your beer and take your order when I return."

"You're not supposed to order until after they serve our drinks," Malinda chided. They had dined out together a hundred times and Jared usually practiced proper dining etiquette, but tonight he was acting out, demonstrating that he was aware of a hidden agenda and he didn't want any part of it.

"I'm hungry," he growled. "You're gonna be hungry after you eat that water bug. You need some meat."

"Excuse me? Water bug?"

"Lobster. It's just a giant water bug. Nasty thing. I wouldn't eat one if you paid me."

Four years ago, Jared had boldly walked into her office unannounced, twisting a piece of paper nervously in his hands. Looking up from her computer screen, Malinda saw kind brown eyes, gorgeous wavy locks, and a killer smile.

"May I help you?" she asked. He nodded and handed her his résumé.

"So, you rodeo?"

"Yes, ma'am. Got pinned under a bronc two months ago and smashed my leg pretty bad. I need a little extra income until I heal up properly."

"But, you don't have any relevant experience. What made you decide to apply at Epitome Architecture?"

He grinned and looked down at the floor. "To tell you the truth, I go to physical therapy on the second floor, and I seen you a couple of times and asked around because I sure would like to work for you." His eyes shone like polished amber.

"Had seen," she corrected.

"Ma'am?"

"Had seen, or saw. Not, seen."

"Oh." He blushed, turning his cowboy hat in circles. "I never was very good in English class."

"Never mind. If you 'asked around,' you must know that this is an architectural firm?"

"Yes, ma'am."

"We design buildings."

"Yes, ma'am."

"You rodeo," she repeated.

"Yes, ma'am. I won the National Finals last year. Saddle bronc. Maybe you've heard of me?" He flashed a brilliant smile that made her want to crawl into his mouth and let him devour her.

"No . . ." she glanced at the sheet of paper in front of her. "Jared Moreno. I'm sorry, I haven't. I don't follow the rodeo circuit."

"That's okay. Right now, I need to favor my leg a little. There's nothing wrong with my arms, though." He innocently flexed his biceps, and she was the one who blushed now.

"I think you might be looking for construction work."

"No, ma'am. I seen . . . I mean, saw . . . watched your gardeners working out front, and they don't do a very good job. One thing I am really good at, besides ridin' buckin' horses, is gardening and taking care of lawns. See there?" he pointed to his résumé. "Kelley's Landscaping and Garden Center. Six years experience. I really like that kind of work. I only quit 'cause I was on the road so much the last couple years."

"We're under contract with a landscaping service," Malinda explained, "but I could use a gardener at my home. I don't have the time or patience to do it, and I've been thinking about hiring someone to help me. This must be fate."

It was a blatant lie.

She loved gardening, had never considered hiring a gardener, did not believe in fate, and never lied—until now. Every spring, she designed a new flowerbed, tilling the soil and painstakingly planting rows of perennials and annuals. Nurturing her seedlings until they burst into a radiant display of color was therapeutic and rewarding. She admired the results of her labor all summer while mourning the loss each fall. With her impulsive fabrication, she knew she had just entered previously unexplored territory—the cougar and the cub.

Jared's skill at landscaping was exactly as he had professed. While Malinda worked at her architectural firm in the inner city, he built a retaining wall, put in a magnificent stone fountain, planted two new gardens, and pruned, pinched back, and primped every plant and bush on the property. She enjoyed gardening as a hobby, but he mastered it.

Malinda found herself looking forward to going home at the end of her workday knowing that Jared would be there to sit with her on the patio and watch the sunset. She laughed at his stories of prize-winning rodeos, hard-drinking cowboys, and the women who followed them, interrupting occasionally to correct his English. On weekends, in her impeccable backyard, he taught her how to throw both a lariat and a football. He took her to an enormous County Western bar where he patiently showed her how to Cotton Eye Joe. Sundays were set aside for fishing at the lake—a sport she never imagined she would learn and enjoy so immensely. She introduced him to wine, gourmet food, foreign films, and reading.

All too soon, a chill crept into the sultry summer air, making an earlier appearance with each passing evening. They both knew his seasonal work was coming to an end, but

Malinda wanted Jared to remain in her life. In one brief discussion, she persuaded him to move out of his studio apartment and into her master bedroom. His brightly colored shirts and starched Wranglers hung across from Burberry, Chloé, and Marc Jacobs. His three pairs of boots stood in sharp contrast to designer heels organized by color and perched on shoe racks. A year later they were married on a sandy beach in Mexico.

Tonight, she was asking for a divorce. It was inevitable. They were mismatched from the start, and she needed to convince Jared that this was the right decision for both of them. He refused to discuss it at home when she had brought it up two weeks earlier. He had walked out of the house, put on headphones, and started up the riding lawnmower. She felt deceitful asking for a divorce at their favorite restaurant, but it had to be done, and hopefully, he wouldn't walk out. With lobster, steak, and wine before them, she began.

"Jared, you know what I want to talk about. This is so hard for me," she choked and blurted out her request. "I want a divorce. We can't go on like this . . . bickering about every little thing. My heart is breaking, but I know it's the right thing to do. We truly have nothing in common and the age difference is just too much for us to reconcile."

"Too much for you," Jared said. "It's never been too much for me. I've told you that so many times. I don't give a rat's ass about the age difference. You're the one who makes a big deal about it. Have I ever, even once, said anything about your age?"

She shook her head.

"No, and I never will. Not now, not ten years from now, not twenty years from now. I married you because I love you. I said vows. Vows that came from my heart. Hell, I even paid a professional to help me write them with the correct grammar so I wouldn't embarrass you. I've lived with you criticizing the way I talk, and I take it because I didn't pay attention in school, and a man should speak proper English. I appreciate learning from you. I wouldn't be drinking this fine glass of Cabernet if it wasn't for you. I didn't know anything existed besides beer, tequila, and whiskey. You've taught me a lot and I'm not done learning. You can't just walk away from your student because you're uncomfortable. Every time I get on a buckin' horse, I'm uncomfortable. I'm scared, and pray I will stay on for eight seconds to make you proud of me. I used to ride because I was a wild crazy kid. Now, I ride for you. And you want to quit?

"You want to throw away our love and caring and years of learning about each other's crazy quirks? Well, I don't. And believe me—you make my hair stand on end sometimes. You are too meticulous. You're hard on yourself and everybody else. You take an hour to get ready for bed and two hours to get ready in the morning."

The waiter returned to refill their drinks and Jared paused. "You throw temper tantrums about things you can't change— like the garbage man, for instance. He doesn't line up the cans the way you like them, and he probably does it because he knows it drives you nuts. He's been doin' it since the day I moved in, but you won't let it go. You want that garbage can to be set up perfectly just like you want our marriage to be perfect, and it's ridiculous."

"I don't think you should compare our marriage to a garbage can."

"I'm not. I'm happy with our marriage, the point is . . . I don't care if it isn't perfect. I try not to be bothered by your borderline obsessive compulsiveness." He saw the surprised expression on her face. "You got me interested in reading and now I read. I know a lot more than you think I do. I'm not a shy, uneducated young man anymore, and I have you to thank for that." He reached across the table and took her hands, looking into her eyes.

"Have I ever said a harsh word to you?"

She shook her head.

"Have I ever hit you or cheated on you?"

Again, she shook her head.

"Am I ugly? You can't stand to look at me? Am I a bad lover?"

She had to stifle a laugh when he said that. They both knew that was far from the truth.

"Then tell me why you want a divorce."

"Because I'm going to be fifty in two years and I can't bear the thought of getting old while you're still so young. You didn't even know how old I was! You've never asked, and I've never told you. Now you know." Tears rolled down her cheeks. "My boobs and butt will sag and I'll get wrinkles and *you* won't be able to look at *me*! You'll leave me for someone your own age or even younger!" There, she had said it. Her fear was as exposed as the lobster she had ripped from its shell and she had never felt more vulnerable.

"Look at me, Malinda." She dabbed her eyes with a napkin and met his gaze. "I've never told you this before, but when I walked into your office four years ago, I already knew how old you were. My sister Googled you. I had been watching you for two weeks, but I didn't want you to think I was a crazy stalker so I never mentioned it. I thought you were the most beautiful woman I ever seen." He grinned and winked at her. "The most beautiful woman I had ever seen, and as I look at you tonight, I still feel the same way. You're not going to look old for a long, long time, and I will never get tired of looking at you because I see your heart and soul. I know where your true beauty is.

"You see people looking at us and you think they're smirking. I see people looking at us and I think they're admiring our courage. You're so defensive about our relationship that you don't see the beauty in it. The beauty of us, together, as a couple. Living up to your expectations is no easy task, but I haven't given up. You've made me a better man, and I'd like to think that I've helped you become a better woman. You're not near as uptight as you were when we first met. You've learned to relax and shake things off, and now you need to learn what is really important in life and stop sweating the small stuff."

"Oh, Jared. I am such an idiot. I love you. I do. I really, really do."

"I know you do. Now, can we please put this age discussion to rest?"

"Yes, I believe we can."

"Promise me you won't bring this up again? Because I really don't care to discuss it again. I don't think I can come up with another speech like that."

"I promise." Her heart was full, saturated with tenderness, joy, and love.

"By the way, I have a surprise," Jared grinned. "That chew I spit out tonight was my last one and that's my promise to you. I'm going to see a hypnotherapist I found online. He's supposed to be really good at helping people with this addiction. It's a nasty habit and I want to be rid of it."

She looked into the sincere, intense brown eyes of the most mature man she had ever known and marveled at how lucky she was. Her fear of aging had almost resulted in her ending a relationship with a remarkable man who appreciated cultural differences, defied social stigma, and openly declared his love for her. They had built a foundation based on their love of learning and unbridled passion, and now it was time for genuine acceptance.

If Jared had agreed to a divorce, the realm of her existence would have been forever altered. She would have lost a vital component in her life and this realization shook her to her very core.

There was no age barrier obstructing their marriage. It was a wall she had put up all on her own. She made another promise, this one to herself. From now on, she was going to embrace the reality of true love between a man and a woman. Cougars and cubs were an illusion.

PHRASED IN THE FORM OF A QUESTION

MARCIA GAYE

Answer: A perpetrator of misconceptions and misdemeanors.

Question: What is Janelle's mirror?

Janelle's reflection represented a version of herself that did not include the horrific divorce, the wayward son, the weight gain, the doubts. The woman in her mirror appeared confident, capable, bordering on attractive. A red V-neck T-shirt perked up her complexion. A henna wash disguised the few grays in her brunette hair. Pleased with the accomplishment of fitting into skinny jeans, the former flower child hardly missed her comfort food or comfort clothes. Flowing maxi dresses and bell-bottoms were exiled to the distant past.

Sitting on the edge of her bed, Jan unlaced the walking shoes with custom arch supports, and slipped into snakeskin kitten heels. Without time to mull over what to wear, fixing her face took priority. With a wave of the magic mascara wand, she settled for a slash of lip-gloss and a spritz of perfume. An invitation had come by way of the phone just minutes ago.

"Hello, Janelle, it's Michael Williams. I feel like cooking. Would you like to come over for an evening breakfast? We can watch *Jeopardy!*."

This little quirk of including his formal name indicated a lack of arrogance that Janelle found endearing. Most young men were clueless about simple gentility. Janelle had answered the phone on occasion to "Yo, it's me," and "Wazzup?"

"Hi, Michael. You know, you don't always have to add Williams. The other Michaels I know go by Mike. So when you say Michael, I know it's you."

"Okay."

She noted the acquiescence in his voice, knew the pale skin behind his ears was turning pink. Janelle smiled.

"Sure. Breakfast is my favorite meal for dinner. Should I bring anything?"

"Real butter, if you have any. I only have margarine. And maybe some jam? Come on over; I'm pre-heating the oven."

Grabbing butter, orange marmalade and door keys, Jan stepped into the elevator. Her reflection greeted her from the chrome side panel. Her hair swung in a high ponytail, the way she wore it around home. She pinched the clasp open and hooked it to her belt buckle. A link on her home page had declared just this morning that men still prefer long, loose hair on women. Maybe she should have paid attention to that kind of detail when she was married.

The woman in the panel could almost pass for Michael's age, though he was sixteen years younger. His intelligence exceeded his years in some areas, proved by his early completion of a meteorology degree. They met a few months before, in the first floor clubroom during a tornado warning. A new face, attached to a well-crafted twenty-something hard body, caught her eye.

"Welcome to the Andover building. Are you settling in okay?" This killer of an opening line wasn't going to make much of a first impression. Impulsive actions had taken her by surprise again. She hadn't thought ahead and silently chided herself for sounding so bland.

"Hello. Fine, thanks. So this is the Midwest's famous tornado alley? Seems more like an excuse for a party." The young man flicked longish blond hair out of his eyes. No ring on his left hand. A great smile. Pale skin like hers—the type that doesn't tan. An evening shadow of reddish stubble over his chin.

"Well, you get used to it. There'll be warnings all summer. So, you're new to the area?" Jan winced a little at this lame version of "Come here often?"

She found out Michael Williams had come to work for the local weather service, relocating from New England. After that first meeting, Janelle had become his partner in a dubious pursuit of amateur storm tracking. More than a few times, they took Michael's pickup outside the city limits and parked, watching the sky for tornado activity. This recklessness produced a thrill deep down in Janelle that she hadn't felt since high school. A feeling as if she had nothing to lose.

If the storm didn't come to them, Janelle insisted they go in search of it. Despite Michael's futile objections, he'd crank the truck into gear and head directly into the wind. One particular excursion almost ended the pattern before it had time to develop fully.

"Listen, I have to pull over. Visibility is impossible. We'll wait it out." He stopped beside a field, and Jan opened her door. "Wait. Where are you going?"

"I just have to feel it, Michael. I want to feel it."

Like a child, she ran in circles, arms up, until all her energy expelled. Then, with nothing to see, she stood, eyes closed. The wind and rain were enough. After what seemed like hours, she felt Michael's hand on her arm and let him guide her back to the truck, then home. She fell asleep under Michael's watch, wet and warm on her living room floor. He was gone when she woke up.

Other times, he stayed longer. With the exuberance of discovery that only the young possess, he could hold a conversation long into the night about weather, music, modern art, or college sports. It was during one of those marathon conversations that Janelle had become aware of whom she might be in Michael's eyes, aware of his focus on the movement of her lips rather than on what she was saying. She paused mid-thought without his realizing it. A tiny gasp caught in her throat as his gaze lowered from lips to neck. Silence in the space between them grew conspicuous, shocking them back into conversation.

He had the same look again the day she wore the blue dress and her legs showed bare next to the gearshift lever in his pickup. That time they were on their way to a lecture about tracing family genealogies. From handed-down stories and names repeated in her family tree, Janelle had decided her ancestors must be Scottish. She hoped to find proof. During the drive to the library, she chattered on about how name spellings were commonly altered due to illiterate interpretations of dialect.

"Williams is a common name though. I doubt you'll have much to wonder about. Your ancestors are most certainly English. Or maybe the name did get altered. Perhaps from German. What have your parents told you?"

"My parents passed when I was in eleventh grade. At that age, I didn't pay much attention. I know where they were born and married, so that's a start." Michael tried to make this revelation sound nothing more than fact, but Jan saw that pale skin behind his ears darken a shade. His eyes stayed on the road.

"Michael, I'm sorry." She paused, giving him a moment to tell her more. He didn't. She put her hand on his shoulder, then slid down the nubby weave of his sleeve, and rested on the hand he kept on the gearshift. His skin burned so hot she quickly drew back.

"Sure, knowing where their births are recorded will be a great start," she recovered nicely. "You can work backward. It shouldn't be hard to trace at least a few generations pretty quickly. I've given my kids printouts so they'll have the information later if they want it. Teenagers have too much else they're interested in. But when they start having kids, they'll want to know, I think."

This new look on Michael's face was miles different from the way he'd been staring at her legs. His neck drained back to white. Jan realized what she'd said and what her sympathetic remarks had revealed. It wasn't as if she'd been hiding her kids. That'd be ridiculous. Their photos were out in plain sight in her apartment.

Michael maintained his *just the facts, Ma'am,* facade. "You haven't told me about your kids. Teenagers?"

"Oh? You've seen their pictures, haven't you? Sure. Sarah and Ian."

"The family pictures on your desk? I figured they were of nieces and nephews. But they're yours." It was phrased as a statement, not a question. His voice trailed off. Then, "Where do they live?"

"Oh, on campus. Well, Ian lives on campus at Ohio State. Sarah is married. She lives in Pennsylvania. They're not really teenagers anymore." Janelle struggled to catch her breath. Then she went for nonchalance. "You might see them over the holidays. Maybe not, though. It's more convenient when we gather at Sarah's."

"And your ex? How long were you married?"

Jan had released her status as divorcée that first night, the same time she'd made sure the handsome meteorologist was single.

"He's gone. I don't know where." This was not how this conversation should go. "Um, twenty-one years. I was a child bride, robbed from my cradle."

"So, you're old enough to . . ."

Janelle stopped him quickly. "I'm old enough to be your aunt." She busted out laughing. What else could she do?

The age revelation hadn't made much difference in their friendship. Living in the same building certainly offered an advantage for a guy too busy with a new career to make many social advances. Impromptu invitations flew back and forth.

A tingle ran up Janelle's spine as the elevator opened on his floor. The feeling pleased and annoyed her at the same time. The little joys she felt with Michael were growing bigger all the time. It was silly to have those thoughts about a guy young enough to be her—favorite nephew. She shook it off and tapped a quick knock on his door.

Their apartments had the same floor plan. Michael had a proper dining room suite placed where she had her home office set up. He was collecting furniture with the plan to buy a house one day, while she had downsized to a desk, sofa, and single bed.

While Michael cooked in his tiny kitchen, Janelle set out dishes from the hutch. The china must have been his mother's. That explained the flowery pattern. Michael brushed past her to reach for a drawer. Too casually, he slipped out some candles, placed them in holders on the table and lit them. The candleholders were a present from Janelle, a welcome gift after he moved in. She had joked that they would add a touch of femininity to his bachelor pad, an aid in his pursuit of young women. The parallel was not lost on Jan. She dimmed the lights a nudge.

Overcooked eggs and too crisp bacon would've caused her to scold herself if she had made them, but by candlelight, with Benny Goodman in the player, the taste didn't seem to matter.

"Your cooking is improving all the time. The gravy is perfect and that's a difficult thing to master. It's nice to relax with some comfort food." Compliments to the cook are always appropriate. It'd be difficult for even Jan to bungle that.

"Glad you think so. I'm practicing for a long winter. When tornado season is over, I'll be advising folks to tuck in for all the comfort they can get. Cabin fever gets pretty severe in New England. What do you do with yourselves here?"

"You seem to have a grasp of the method. Good food, good friends, and a good way to keep warm. All anybody really needs. Simple."

After dinner, sitting on the sofa, they revived their normal friendly competition. Their *Jeopardy!* score was close to being tied as they called out correct questions in response to the answers Alex Trebek read on screen. The *Monarchies of Great Britain* category gave Jan a chance to show off. Michael's best chance hinged on *Bits About Big Bands.* Obviously, Michael had been born long after the Big Band era, but he enjoyed a sizeable CD collection of the music. He often loaned Janelle what they didn't listen to together.

Louis Armstrong's *A Kiss to Build a Dream On* had become one of her favorites. She sang it in the shower. She sang it in the car. She hummed it at night as she slipped into sleep. She didn't consider it might be one of Michael's favorites too. Not until Alex answered, "*It* will make that dream come true." They sang out in unison, "What is *my imagination?*"

Suddenly Janelle lost concentration on the game. The phrase played in her mind over and over, and she found herself wondering. Again. If she caught the exact moment, she could phrase it just right, in the form of a question. *Michael, would you give me just one kiss? I ask no more than this, just a kiss to build a dream on.*

She dared not turn her head but considered him in her peripheral vision. Heat emanated from him. Moisture glistened under his hairline, darkening the blond wisps. She imagined her fingers lifting his hair, steam rising as she gently blew on his skin.

"What is *a clarinet?*" his question erupted next to her. And she imagined how his lips would purse as he blew into a clarinet.

It was some minutes later that the clarinet music in her thoughts morphed into the countdown theme, that instantly recognizable tick-tocking interlude of the *Final Jeopardy!* sequence. Michael shifted forward on the sofa, closer to the screen. Janelle had missed the category, but there it was in blazing color: *December/May Romance.*

"It's *Mary Tyler Moore*, right? She married that younger doctor." Michael turned to Janelle for agreement so she nodded.

"You know, you have that kind of smile, like Mary's."

Janelle attempted to respond but her words sputtered and slipped away. A reflexive, nervous smile opened on her lips.

"There, see? That's it. That pretty smile." Michael curved his fingers under her chin and tipped it up until their eyes met.

Their smiles matched and as his lips blended into hers, she had the perfect answer to her unasked question.

They didn't see which TV contestant became champion, but Janelle felt herself the true winner of more than just a game.

THERAPEUTIC INK

KATHRYN COIT

Patricia wasn't sure what to expect of "Camp Victory," a weekend retreat for women cancer survivors, sponsored by a local charity. All she knew for certain was that she needed to do something different after reaching the five-year mark this spring. She was feeling at loose ends most of the time these days. Maybe she could get some ideas from others who'd felt this way. And even if she didn't, it would be a great break from her normal routine.

She had arrived at the conference center the previous evening, enjoyed an excellent lasagna dinner, and met her roommates afterward at the movie shown outside under the stars. Now it was time to choose her breakout sessions for the day. A free massage following lunch certainly sounded appealing! "How long has it been since somebody did something that nice for you?" she asked another woman sitting nearby.

"I know what you mean," Sherry answered. "It's always about needles and scans and medicines and symptoms. Those massages sound heavenly! I signed up for that the very first thing."

Pat had always enjoyed music of many types, so the evening concert by a young Italian tenor should be a definite winner. From the CD cover printed in the brochure, he appeared to be easy on the eyes, as well.

"I've seen him perform before," Sherry said. "Bring a glass of wine and prepare to settle in for sheer relaxation. He's great." In her free time in the afternoon, Patricia was really looking forward to a long walk around the lake. The forecast was for 70 degrees, the birds were singing, and lilacs were in bloom. She hadn't been out of the city in months and simply being out in nature again was already beginning to help her unwind.

That left only the decision about the morning session to be made. In high school, Patricia had enjoyed creative writing and that was definitely something she had not found time for in recent years, so she decided to participate in the journaling group. It seemed like a good idea until she had made several false starts and succeeded only in thoroughly frustrating herself.

"I was very young when I was born, and it seems like such a long time ago," she began, "Good grief, how stupid!"

"I've been a nurse for over thirty years, and I enjoy helping people," she tried next, "How sappy!"

Well, then, Patricia thought, *how about, I've been knocked down many times, but I'm still here*. That one, she decided, sounded so self-serving she wouldn't even want to keep it in a totally private journal. After several more minutes of searching for a starting point, tearing pages out of her notebook and throwing them away, and becoming increasingly convinced she had lost any writing talent she may have ever had, Pat quietly walked out of the room.

"If this is going to help me figure out what to do with the rest of my life, since it looks like I'm going to be around for it," she muttered, "I'm going to have to do better than that."

"Too restless to write?" one of her roommates, Lori, asked. She had just come out of the craft room, proudly showing off her first completed project of the morning.

"You got it," Pat replied with a grin. "And, believe me, I am not a crafty person, so that doesn't look like fun at all! I love your bracelet, but if I have to make it for myself it ain't a gonna happen! Give me a bag of all those beads and tell me to string them up, and I might string you up instead," she laughed.

"Okay, I believe you," Lori said. "Think I'll move on to safer ground. See you at lunch."

Checking her retreat schedule, Patricia found that only one morning break-out session hadn't begun yet—"Therapeutic Ink: Tattoos and Treatment." The description of the session claimed it "would support the notion that tattoos can provide relief for individuals suffering from a number of different mental health concerns and problems, including grief and loss, depression, anxiety, and chronic disease."

Tattoos as a 'therapeutic intervention'? Pat thought sarcastically. *In all my years in the medical field, I've sure never heard that one before! Is it like people who claim to get relief from their emotional pain by cutting themselves, or something? This is nuts!* The more she thought about it, though, the more curious she became. Besides that, it was still too cool outside to take an early walk or sit out on the patio and read. So what did she really have to lose?

Patricia found the appropriate room and a seat in the far back corner, just in case she wanted to slip out again—and was amazed to find the topic intriguing. The presenter shared examples of body art that had been done as memorials to lost loved ones, or in honor of special people, situations or anniversaries. He stressed that tattooing has become much more accepted in the mainstream over recent years, and that it is completely safe if properly done. It wasn't that Pat hadn't heard this repeatedly from young family members who sported multiple "tats," but it just sounded more convincing from a professional.

As she had expected, Pat thoroughly enjoyed the rest of the weekend's events, especially the closing praise service on Sunday morning and the "thanksgiving" lunch. She had met some people she would never forget, and knew she would try her best to attend again in upcoming years. But the big surprise of the weekend was that the tattoo idea was the one thing that wouldn't leave her mind.

Patricia decided that her body had failed her in many ways over the years—not just the cancer but her never-ending battle with her weight and other health issues—but the one perfect thing, the one thing she wanted to permanently acknowledge and record, was that she had given birth to three children who were her entire world.

So, a couple of weeks later, despite years of disapproving of such things, Pat found herself at a tattoo parlor not far from her home. She felt a bit like she should be going in disguise, peering over her shoulder for anyone who would recognize her, or sneaking in the back door. When the young man looked up from behind the counter to greet her, she nearly turned and ran back out to the street! *And then how foolish will you look?* she reminded herself. *You've come this far. Go for it!*

The process was definitely painful, but she was happy with the results, her kids' names linked with daisies around her wrist like a bracelet—and it didn't hurt at all that the guy who gave her the body art was so cute! He tried to keep her laughing so she wouldn't notice the process, and she realized it had been a long time since she had done something for herself or been in the presence of a handsome attentive male. How could he not be attentive—he had to hold her hand for two hours! This was so different from being "mom" or being "hey, nurse" or even spending time with a girlfriend. This was a whole new experience and she was seeing things in an entirely different way than she had before.

Patricia enjoyed this appointment with Greg so much that she went back to the shop for another tattoo a few weeks later. This time she had him give her a small teal ribbon on her ankle, in acknowledgement of ovarian cancer and in support of research toward a cure. Patricia and Greg chatted throughout the whole procedure about anything and everything, and she really hated to leave when it was completed.

So, after another few weeks, Pat worked up the courage to go back yet again, for a larger tattoo this time. Greg tried to convince her to get a "tramp stamp" and promised he would make it perfect for her.

"You have got to be kidding," Patricia laughed. "You may be my favorite gorgeous young man, and you may have a heart of gold, and I may be having a blast visiting you here like this, but you are not about to get that close to my backside with your eyeballs or with your tattoo gun!"

"Okay, okay, you can't blame me for trying," he said with a wink. "It would be cute."

"Cute, my . . . no I can't say that," Pat said, grinning, "that's the whole point!"

Greg and Patricia finally reached agreement on a butterfly on her shoulder, a universally recognized symbol of new life, with plans to add dogwood blossoms around it the next month.

"When you came in for that first tattoo, so unsure of yourself and almost suspicious acting," Greg laughed, giving Pat a hug, "I never dreamed I'd see you in here again in a million years. You are becoming quite the tattoo addict!"

"I am most definitely not addicted to this stuff!" Pat shot back. "You know I just love to hear about that precious little girl of yours and everything that's going on in your life, and this is the perfect opportunity to have a captive audience with you. I've enjoyed watching you work and visiting with you enough to put up with the tattoos, that's all."

"Right, right. There are other ways to spend time together, you know," Greg responded. "How about we go get a pizza together after I get cleaned up here?"

"Are you sure you have time for a date with an old gal like me?" Patricia asked. "Won't somebody be waiting for you at home? I don't want to get you in trouble."

"It will be fine," Greg said. "I'll just give Maggie a call and let her know that I'll be getting home late tonight. Where do you want to eat, Mom?"

A Worker's Compensation

Sonia Todd

Elizabeth heard her cell phone buzz on the nightstand. She had set it on vibrate to keep it from waking her too early, which she noted mentally, did not work. She peeked at the clock with half open eyes. It glowed 1:45 a.m. Elizabeth groaned as her phone shuddered and shook on the nightstand again. She reached for the device with closed eyes, fumbling in blindness.

"Hello," Elizabeth said groggily.

"Sorry to bother you Liz, but . . ." Rachel her assistant said perkily.

"Do you know what time it is?" Elizabeth interrupted.

"Well, here it is 10:45 p.m. and also the first time I have worked later than you in eight years. I know I should have waited until morning to call, but we have a small crisis in R&D and a big crisis in marketing."

"Okay." Elizabeth rolled over on her elbow and let out a sigh. She squinted against the little bit of light filtering into the room around the closed curtains and rubbed her temples. "Couldn't this wait until I was awake on East Coast time?"

"Well R&D wants to know if we are going with an alternate power supply, marketing needs to know if you want to go with mock-up one or two, and Castlemeyer announced the new CFO this morning. The guy will be here Thursday so you need to get back ASAP."

Suddenly Elizabeth was fully awake, her eyes shot open and she sat straight up in bed.

"I thought he was waiting until next month!"

"The Wilson group was ready to make an offer and Castlemeyer was afraid if he didn't move first, he would lose this guy. So he put the bait out and the new guy snapped it up. He'll be here early Thursday."

"You know he will essentially be the new head of the company. At some point you're going to have to stop calling him 'the new guy.' What *is* his name anyway?"

"His name is Martenson. He comes from a small tech company out of Rhode Island that grew 300% under his leadership."

"I need to get a flight . . ."

"Already done. I got you on the red-eye tomorrow out of JFK, you will be touching down at LAX by 1:30, and I will be there to pick you up."

"Get everything you can on this guy and be ready to brief me in the car."

"I'm on it, boss."

Elizabeth hung up and got out of bed. The next several hours whizzed by as Elizabeth prepared for her early departure and wrapped up the loose ends of her trip. By 3:30 a.m., she had sent forty-seven emails, fifteen text messages, and eighteen phone calls that had all gone to voice mail. She couldn't sleep knowing there was work to do.

When Castlemeyer had hired her as V.P. of infrastructure, she had set out to prove herself. As the only female executive at the company, she had felt an overwhelming pressure to be more, to be better, and to show that hiring a woman was not a mistake. Elizabeth made a reputation of being tough but fair, and worked harder than any of her counterparts. Her commitment and zeal had not gone unnoticed by Castlemeyer, the great-great-great grandson of the company's creator. He had awarded Elizabeth with annual bonuses, awards, atta-boys and more work. Now he was hiring someone above her, the only executive in the company with a higher rank, and she would have someone new to impress.

The last CFO had finally stepped-down after ten years and Elizabeth recognized her chance for the higher position but had been passed over. *Probably for some geriatric good-ol'-boy club member,* Elizabeth mused. *Likely, some ancient throwback from the FDR administration who would call her 'Betts' or 'Hon' and wink at her and ask her to get the coffee.* She refused to play secretary to this 'new guy' as Rachel called him. By the time this Martenson got into work, she would be well ahead of him, even if she had to run all the way back to Los Angeles from Manhattan in Christian Louboutin pumps and a Gucci business suit.

Around four in the morning, Elizabeth took a shower and tried to wash off the stress of the day. By the time she was dressed, it was time to leave for the airport. The plane was unusually crowded for an early morning flight. Elizabeth sighed inwardly and braced herself for the claustrophobic passage. The seat Rachel had secured for her was in coach, located in front of a family of five coming back from their first vacation to the Big Apple. The small child located in the seat directly behind her was singing a song from the musical CATS, and off-key at that.

Before the airplane taxied toward the runway Elizabeth could feel the singing child begin to rhythmically kick her seat. Her chair bounced back and forth almost in tune with the throbbing in her head. She gave a pleading look to the flight attendant four rows ahead that was starting beverage service. Elizabeth found herself secretly praying for alcohol in the beverage cart.

As the flight attendant approached, Elizabeth could see her scowling. The attendant was curt when she approached Elizabeth and said, "Ma'am we need to see you for a moment. Please collect your personal belongings and come with me."

"But . . ."

"This way please," the attendant directed.

Elizabeth gathered her carry-on and followed the woman toward the front of the plane past the miniature kitchenette and through the sacred curtain of first class.

"I found you a new seat," the attendant began "I didn't mean to scare you, but I saw that little devil kicking your chair for six straight minutes and thought if it was driving me crazy, it must be driving you crazy also. Welcome to your new seat."

Elizabeth thanked her profusely and began to settle into her new seat. When she had a minute to look out the window she sighed.

"Bumped to first class? Must be your lucky day."

Elizabeth was startled by the male voice next to her. "Yeah, I guess so," was all she could muster.

She looked at the man squarely, wondering if he was trying to be engaging or rude. He appeared younger than she did and wore a tailored suit. She guessed he was in sales by his starched smile. Elizabeth routinely flew thousands of miles a month and it was unusual to find someone who wanted to chat on a flight, she was suspicious of his intentions. *I swear,* Elizabeth thought, *if this guy tries to sell me insurance or annuities I am going back to the chair-kicking kid.*

"So are you traveling for business or pleasure?" The man asked.

Here comes the sales pitch, Elizabeth said to herself, but she replied, "Business."

"Me too," the man said. "So what do you do?"

Elizabeth did not want to invite more questions, so she was purposefully vague, "Oh, a little of this and a little of that."

"Me too," the man smiled wryly.

Elizabeth couldn't help herself; she decided to shut down the conversation, "Yeah, I used to be a professional eater. I can eat thirty-nine hot dogs in under two minutes. But my sister was injured in a freak bologna accident, so I gave up the gluttonous life and joined the circus."

The stranger openly smiled, stifling a laugh. "No kidding?" And without missing a beat the man continued, "Well I was an Elvis impersonator for ten years until my hips gave out. Then I became a semi-pro Atari gamer. My specialty is Pong. But my dream has always been the exotic world of tattoo art; I have been practicing on citrus fruit."

Elizabeth laughed out loud and several passengers turned to stare. The man stuck out his hand, "William."

Elizabeth took his hand and shook it, "Elizabeth."

"Can I call you Betsy?"

"Only if I can call you Billy."

"How about Beth?"

"Okay. Bill?"

"Nice to meet you."

"Likewise."

"Welcome to first class."

"Thank you. I didn't think it was actually possible to get bumped up, but it did save a child from being thrown into the upper atmosphere."

"Aha. Well, lucky kid, lucky me." He smiled warmly at Elizabeth and she uncharacteristically blushed. "So, what other hobbies do you have when you aren't charming strangers and saving children from being hurled into the ozone?"

"Panic mostly. You?"

"That about sums it up."

The flight attendant came around with refreshments and they both ordered the vegetable quiche and juice.

William held up his glass of O.J. and said, "A toast, to nice surprises."

It wasn't like Elizabeth to be openly flirting with a total stranger. She blamed it on her hellish morning, lack of sleep, and impending stress. Still, it was nice to relax and take a brief diversion from real life. She couldn't remember the last time she had laughed, or hadn't thought about work. Rachel, and anyone else who knew her, would be shocked at the way she was carrying on. Teasing like a school girl, with a gorgeous, and funny, man that she would guess was at least ten years her junior. She shook her head internally and promised herself when the plane landed there would be no more nonsense; it would be back to business as usual.

William and Elizabeth talked for the rest of the flight. The conversation flowed without awkward silences or useless posturing. When the plane landed and they parted ways, Elizabeth was genuinely sad to see him go. It was the most enjoyable morning she had spent in recent memory and the closest thing to a date she had experienced in years.

"You asked for his number?" Rachel screeched when Elizabeth retold the story later.

"I wanted to see him again." Elizabeth shrugged, as if her pursuing a man was a daily occurrence.

"Didn't he have a business card?" Rachel asked with only half-hidden suspicion.

"No, he said he was in between jobs."

"You have been out of the game for a while so let me explain something to you: 'between jobs' is code for 'unemployed.'"

"He was flying first class."

"Well, did he actually give you his number?" Rachel folded her arms defiantly.

"He doesn't have a phone yet. He just moved here." Elizabeth shuffled papers on her desk and refused to make eye contact.

"Everyone has a phone. My ten-year-old neighbor has two cell phones! He is obviously hiding something. Like maybe a wife!"

"I gave him my number. You'll see when you meet him. He is a really neat guy."

"Neat? Are you insane? He's probably a hit-man or something."

"He was wearing a suit. Besides, having plausible reasons for his behavior does not make him a psycho-path-out-of-work-married-ex-con. Now let's just drop the whole thing. Besides he said he would be really busy for the next few weeks, and so will we."

"Married," Rachel muttered. Elizabeth glared at her. "Sorry." Rachel turned her eyes back to the stack of papers in front of her. "I'm working, I'm working."

Elizabeth had Rachel running on her first day back in the office. Her mantra was *we only have two days to prepare.* Other than coffee and the occasional salad, she didn't even break for sustenance. At 4:30 her cell phone rang, and she glanced at it but didn't recognize the number. Elizabeth tossed the cell phone at Rachel and said, "Answer that for me?"

Rachel answered, and then began grinning. "No, this is Rachel. Would you like to talk to her?"

Elizabeth overheard and lifted her head from the desk to look at Rachel quizzically. Rachel handed over the phone and Elizabeth said, "Hello" into the receiver. Her face lit up and she began talking in a sing-song voice. Rachel had no idea what the conversation was about but she guessed it was good news the way Elizabeth was acting and kept saying sure, and great, and finished with I can't wait. When Elizabeth hung-up the phone she immediately closed the screen on her laptop. "Rachel, it is time to close shop for the day."

"But it's only 4:30!"

"Yes, but you worked through lunch."

"I always work through lunch."

"Well then, you deserve a break."

"What is going on?"

"I have a-uh . . . meeting I need to get to."

A flicker of understanding crossed Rachel's face, "You're going on a date? Now?" Elizabeth packed up her bag and refused to look at Rachel. "That was *'the guy'* on the phone wasn't it? The young one, from the plane?"

"Yes," was all Elizabeth said.

"You know, this is a really bad idea. We have a ton of work to do." Rachel put her hands on her hips like an accusing mother, "Have you even wondered why a young guy would be interested in an older woman?"

Elizabeth stopped cold; she wanted to be insulted but she couldn't muster the energy. "I was wondering if he was after my money, but then I realized I have it all wrapped up in my retirement accounts and my pre-purchased plot at the cemetery.

So, my hope is that he is after my body." And with that, she left the office.

William met Elizabeth downtown, and they had dinner at a café that had an open mic night. Several patrons went on stage to read poetry, sing, play an instrument or tell jokes.

"This is great, really, I am enjoying this." William said. "I have been to L.A. several times on business but have never seen anything other than the inside of a hotel or conference room."

"I have lived here for most of my life, and I never do this kind of stuff either. Over three decades and never once have I purchased a map of the stars' homes."

"Disneyland?"

"Nope."

"Zoo? Knottsberry Farm? Universal Studios?"

"No. No. And no."

"Well, what do you do?"

"Work."

"Me too. But I have decided a tiger can change its stripes."

"I guess."

Bill tilted his head, "You don't think it is possible, or you don't see the reason to?"

Elizabeth looked at him, "Both. Neither. I don't know. I guess there are things I missed out on for work. But I would have missed out on other things if I hadn't been working. Besides, what else would I do with my time? Knit? Embroider some hand towels? Throw Tupperware parties?"

"Hmmm, I like the Tupperware idea. I have always thought of plastic as very sexy, not sure about the other two."

Elizabeth took a deep breath and asked, "How old are you?"

William feigned embarrassment and covered his chest with his hands. "Well, I never! Don't you know it's not polite to ask a man his age?"

Elizabeth stifled a giggle and said, "Seriously, I know I'm older than you. I am, let's say curious, about why you aren't out with some twenty-year-old aspiring starlet?"

William straightened his jaw, and looked at Elizabeth with interest. He said nothing for a long moment, and Elizabeth wondered if she had insulted him. Finally, he said, "I would rather be with a woman who knows her own worth, than with one who is always trying to prove she is worth something."

Elizabeth felt a warmth that started in her toes and ran all the way up her back like a pleasant electric shock. "So the age difference doesn't bother you?"

"Should it?"

"It's just . . ." Elizabeth trailed off.

"What? It bothers you?"

"No." Elizabeth paused, "If you are after my money, I don't have any."

William knew she was joking and went right back into the companionable mode, "Well, I don't know, there is that whole Tupperware idea you were tossing around. Plastic containers that burp, I see dollar signs." They both laughed, and the evening ended on a high note.

By Thursday morning, Elizabeth had been keeping odd hours. Elizabeth had trouble sleeping the night before, but finally dozed off when the sun came up. Even though she was tired, she woke up smiling. She knew that the changes in the company were serious, the current project a veritable pitfall of problems, and the fact that she didn't care about either, truly problematic. She had no idea what to do about any of it.

"You smile all the time. Ever since you returned from New York you look like a cast member from *Sesame Street*."

"Huh?" Elizabeth asked Rachel absently.

"All sunshine and smiles. What is going on with you?"

"Nothing . . . I'm just . . . nothing."

"What? Is it the homeless guy?"

Elizabeth looked up from her computer screen, "Homeless? He's not homeless."

"Oh, yeah, how do you know? He may have a lovely cardboard box under the bridge downtown."

"No, he has a lovely three bedroom walk-up ten blocks from my apartment."

"Oh, really?"

"Yes." Elizabeth said and blushed.

"O. M. G.! Are you serious?"

"Y.E.S." Elizabeth spelled out. "But all I did was see the inside, so don't get the wrong idea."

"Really?"

"He made dinner for me, if you must know. He is a great cook, and he really did just move here. He's not homeless."

"Well isn't this an interesting development?"

Elizabeth propped her elbows on the desk and rested her chin on her hands. She stared out the window dreamily. "Hmmm," was her response.

"Well, I don't mean to rain on your parade, but we have a board meeting in thirty minutes. *New guy* will be here, and you are acting like a twitter-pated teenager. I am going to say something I never hoped to say, and that I never want to say again in my life." Rachel inhaled sharply and continued in a raised voice, "Get back to work!"

Elizabeth chuckled as she lifted her head lazily from her hands and said, "Yes, boss," and gave Rachel a salute.

Before the board meeting, Elizabeth prepared in every way she knew how. She gathered the necessary documents and said a small prayer. When the corporate change was first announced Elizabeth was angry and hurt; now those feelings had dissipated to disinterest. She didn't feel the rush and thrill of impressing someone new and silently wondered if there was a way to get out of the meeting altogether. In the middle of her daydream, Rachel poked her head in the door, "They are about to start. You ready?"

Elizabeth picked up her papers and headed down the hall to the boardroom. Most of the other execs were there already; several of them gathered around a central figure, presumably, *the new guy*. Elizabeth set down her sheaf of papers and tried to decide if she should enter the fray or wait. Then she heard Castlemeyer say, "Well, there she is. This is who I wanted you to meet."

Since there were no other women in the room, Elizabeth knew Castlemeyer was referring to her, and prepared herself by plastering on a fake smile and extending her hand for the obligatory handshake.

Castlemeyer went on talking to a man that Elizabeth could only see from the back. "This is the one person who will make your job easier—Elizabeth Anderson! She is a tiger and works harder than all of these other fellas combined."

Elizabeth didn't have time to absorb Castlemeyer's compliment, because when Martenson turned around she recognized her new boss. It was William, the man she had kissed goodnight only fourteen hours before.

The two of them stood staring at each other, hands outstretched but not touching. Finally, William gathered his composure and clasped Elizabeth's palm while saying, "Nice to meet you."

Elizabeth stumbled on her "you too" and it came out sounding like "ooo goo" instead. Elizabeth was at a loss and didn't know how to proceed with the entire executive board watching their exchange.

All of a sudden, William said, "I have big plans for this company. I look forward to working with you and hearing your ideas."

Elizabeth couldn't help herself, "Well, I do have this one idea involving Tupperware . . ."

The other executives exchanged glances but William said, "The plastic containers that burp?"

Elizabeth smiled and said, "Yeah, those are the ones."

William smiled and said, "Great, let's have a lunch meeting to discuss that."

Rock the Cradle

E. B. Davis

When the waiter came to her table and asked if she wanted another drink, Lillian Foster said no. A glance at her watch confirmed that it was 10:30 p.m. Reconnecting with Phil, her now-divorced high school beau, had occurred through a happenstance meeting online. Although she had decided to start dating again, she didn't know if they had anything in common after so many years. She only had agreed to a quick drink. *It could be fun, remembering old times,* Lillian thought, *and who knew? He still might be hot.*

The evening hadn't started well. Rock the Cradle's concert at the Civic Center, located near the restaurant, made parking spaces as scarce as sexy fifty-something-year-old men. If the concert hadn't been sold out by the time she discovered Rock the Cradle's schedule, she would have attended since she'd been a fan for two decades. So when Phil asked to meet her, specifying this restaurant, she'd forgotten about the concert and the parking issue it caused. And now he was a half-hour late. For old times' sake, she would remain seated for another fifteen minutes.

Bored, she stared at the table's flowered centerpiece, losing herself in memory. Her husband's casket lowered into the ground. She felt the spring day's rawness and her footfalls on the spongy graveyard. The cemetery's trees in blossom, death feeding new life. The simultaneous horror and beauty of life's cycle.

How had she become a widow at fifty-two? Jeremy's death had happened so suddenly, and yet eight months had passed since the funeral. She coped, stayed busy with her exercise routine and volunteered for the Special Olympics, but she took a break from practicing law. She had begun to reemerge from her cocoon of grief, ready to open herself to new experiences. *Without Jeremy.*

An unfamiliar voice intruded into her thoughts. "Hey Lill. How are you?" a strange man asked, patting her shoulders.

She stared at him. *Who was this stranger?* "Phil?" Lillian asked, half wanting the man to contradict her.

"I'd know you anywhere. You've barely changed," the man said, confirming the now bald paunchy man who had once been a long-haired hunk was, in fact, Phil. He sat down with a thud in the chair opposite hers.

Had his knees given out when he sat? Lillian watched him and rearranged the place setting. "Good to see you again, Phil."

"You're looking mighty hot."

"Thanks," Lillian said. As if on autopilot, she had dressed in black leather pants and boots, topped by a knit blouse and a silk vest. Her wishful-thinking mind, that part of her wanting to be at the concert, had dressed her. But it was nice of Phil to compliment her. Even if she had missed the concert, she could still pull off the music scene look.

"Sorry I'm late. I had a business dinner meeting in the private dining room, which ran late. Meeting you here was convenient. And then my son-in-law called. My daughter went into labor."

"She's having the baby tonight? Phil, you could have cancelled. I would have understood."

"I didn't know. Besides, it's her first child so it may take hours."

"I imagine every grandchild is a treasure."

"Don't you have grandkids?"

"No, Jeremy and I didn't have children."

"How come?"

What an intrusive, insensitive jackass. "We didn't want children." That was the reason she always gave to dunderheads. Fibroids had ended the notion of children for her. But she refused to explain things that were no one's business.

"Oh, I had no idea you didn't want children. Guess we wouldn't have been such a great match way back when. Doesn't matter now, of course."

She wondered if Phil would have been one of those men who wanted children so badly that he would have divorced her to obtain a reproductive mate. *Ick!* A patina of tarnish damaged Phil's memory in her mind, so when the waiter passed by their table, she caught his attention and asked for another Chablis. When Phil asked for a lite beer, Lillian noticed that he sucked in his gut.

"What do you do, Phil?"

"Insurance. Life, whole and term, auto, house, business liability, workmen's compensation, marine and Fireman's."

"Oh . . . how interesting."

"So, you're a widow now. What did your husband do? And yourself?"

"Jeremy was," she faltered, "I'm an entertainment lawyer. My husband and I were partners. Since he died, I haven't had the heart to go back to work . . . at least not yet."

"What's an entertainment lawyer?"

"We represent musicians, actors, and other artists, negotiating contracts and providing legal advice on other matters."

"So, who are your clients?" Phil thrust his upper body over the table and hovered near the table's centerpiece.

"We have many famous entertainers as clients. As you must be aware, client confidentiality bars me from talking about them." Naming clients didn't break professional ethics, but Phil's interest seemed more like an eager adolescent girl living vicariously through the latest pop star.

"Oh come on, Lill. Give me the dirt."

"No dirt. My clients and firm are very professional."

"My youngest daughter went to the Rock the Cradle concert tonight."

"I wanted to attend, too."

"Are you another woman mesmerized by Adam Dresher?"

"Sure, he's a hunk. But their music is great, so passionate."

Phil rolled his eyes. "Speak of the devil. There he is with some twenty-something groupie."

Lillian turned to where Phil was looking. Sure enough, Adam Dresher stood at the bar. His long auburn locks, fine body and rugged face captured her attention. The expression on Adam's face conveyed annoyance as he glanced at those seated. When his eyes found hers, they lit up, and he smiled. Lillian smiled back, her heart rate zooming. She felt heat rise to her face.

"Hello. Remember me?" Phil said. "I'd appreciate if you could focus on me."

"Oh, for heaven sake, Phil. I agreed to a drink, not to be shackled to you."

"If you can't give me your undivided attention for five minutes, there's no point."

"Probably not, Phil. But you need to be with your family tonight anyway."

Phil went silent. The veins stood out on his neck. "Nice knowing you. My wife at least pays attention to me. Screw you!" he said in a loud voice. When Lillian didn't respond, Phil got up from the table and stormed out of the restaurant.

Lillian laughed. Of course, her first attempt at dating after Jeremy's death turned out to be with a lying, married man. Murphy's Law set a precedent when Jeremy died, so why wouldn't it apply to Phil? She wondered if meeting her at the restaurant, where his business engagement took place, had camouflaged their date from his wife. Now that she thought about his behavior, she recalled his possessiveness, inappropriate given the situation. "Mistake" was written all over the evening. *What a skunk!*

Until Jeremy died, her life had been a rich stew of interesting people, a solid marriage, a successful profession, and her philanthropic activities. She had no need to revisit the past.

She turned her attention to Adam Dresher, who still stood at the bar. He looked at her again and smiled. His eyes trailed to the door of the restaurant where Phil had disappeared. She lifted her eyebrows and gestured to the empty chair at her table. He raised his index finger as if asking her to wait a minute.

Lillian ordered an Irish coffee and looked out a nearby window. She noticed people hustling on the sidewalks and through the streets. Glancing at her watch again, she was amazed that the time was eleven-thirty. Most concerts ended at eleven due to a city ordinance, which explained Adam's appearance at the bar.

When the waiter slipped the check in front of her, she realized that Phil hadn't given her any money to pay his share. Lillian laughed again. Another joke on her; it figured.

"Is there a problem, ma'am?" the waiter asked.

"No, not at all, just a joke I remembered."

When the waiter left, her thoughts returned to her marriage. Jeremy had been a creative and energetic partner. Without him, she felt sad and incomplete, but not insecure. *Unchallenged perhaps?* She wondered if Adam had those same characteristics. After twenty years, he still wrote great music and performed for sold-out crowds.

Turning toward the bar, Lillian saw that Adam was arguing with the woman who had accompanied him. The scantily clad woman stood up, said a few terse words that Lillian couldn't hear, then marched out of the restaurant. Adam rolled his eyes, said a few words to the bartender, picked up his drink and walked toward her.

Magnificent!

Adam's hand brushed lightly over her shoulder, making her shiver, then he was at her side.

"We've met before," he said.

Lillian's gaze traveled up from the man's narrow hips at eye level, to his hardened abs defined beneath a black T-shirt, to wide shoulders and a cradle tattoo on his bulging left bicep. Her journey ended at his gorgeous forty-something face crowned with flowing hair.

"Yes, we met briefly at the Special Olympics' fundraiser in New York last year." Her breathlessness made her voice soft and sexy to her own ears.

"May I join you?" Adam asked.

She took a deep breath and cleared her throat. "Of course. I'm surprised to see you here. Did the concert just end?"

Adam sat in the chair next to hers. "Yeah. A friend of mine owns this restaurant, and I promised him I'd stop by. Unfortunately, one of the hangers-on tailed me here."

"Hangers-on?"

"People who consider themselves friends of the band. I think that gal may have screwed Byron, our drummer, a few months ago. Now she's hitting on me."

Lillian grinned. "And you don't like that?"

"No, not particularly. After twenty years, that scene gets old, and having a lot of people backstage just adds to my performance anxiety."

"You seem so self assured. I'm surprised."

"Once I get on stage, I'm fine. But before a show, I still get keyed-up. Our fans deserve our best."

"It's a lot of pressure, isn't it?"

"Yeah, but then, meeting someone like you helps me destress." He smiled.

Lillian's skin temperature rose. He was so hot! She looked him in the eye, and put her hand on his forearm. "The concert sold out before I could get tickets. I missed it." Lillian feigned a pout.

"You like our music?"

"Love it. Have for years."

"Thanks." Adam's forehead crinkled. "It wasn't just the Special Olympics. I've seen you or maybe a picture of you before. I never forget a beautiful woman."

Was he interested? Lillian's heart pounded like a tom-tom. She wondered if he could hear it and longed to rest her head on his chest to hear his. "I'm an entertainment lawyer. My late husband and I were partners."

"What's your name?"

"Lillian Foster."

"Of course, Lillian and Jeremy Foster. I thought about switching to your firm a year ago when my firm gouged me." He took her hand and kissed her knuckles.

His kiss shot through her like a lightning bolt. He didn't release her hand after the waiter brought her Irish coffee. His fingers were long and strong, the mark of a musician. Resting his arm on the table, he held her hand on the tabletop.

"Make that another," he said to the waiter. When they were once again alone, Adam looked Lillian in the eye. "Jeremy died earlier this year, didn't he?"

"Yes. I haven't gone back to work yet. They say the first year is the hardest."

"I can't imagine, but that sounds right. I'm sorry for your loss."

"Thank you. With time, you realize that you must go on. Life doesn't stop. I feel as if I'm living my life in clichés. One door closes, another opens. And just tonight, a little Thomas Wolfe—you can't go home again."

"When I write lyrics that sound cliché, I stop writing and travel, go boarding, do something new to refresh my batteries, especially something physically challenging."

As he spoke, his eyes glimmered with excitement and a zest for life Lillian had seen only in Jeremy's eyes. She remembered how that zeal had attracted her, fascinated her, and she reacted as she had then—as if drawn to a magnet. Adam's speaking voice, just as craggy and beautiful as his voice in song, reverberated down her spine. When he leaned closer to her, she responded, unconsciously mirroring his movement until their sides touched. Her body began to hum.

"So, if you're living in clichés, you must be ready to start a new adventure," he said.

His blue eyes beckoned her to meet his challenge. "Yes, that's probably so. Like wind gone from my sails,"—she laughed at the cliché—"finding direction isn't easy now. I'll have to think about a new adventure."

He bent down and whispered in her ear. "Can I rock your boat?"

Lillian knew she was vulnerable. "Rock, but don't sink."

He brushed her bangs out of her eyes. Then, he placed his hand under her chin and looked her in the eye. "I understand. I'm not like that."

"No promises," she said.

"None given. Are you going to attend the next fundraiser in Boston, week after next?"

"I received the invitation, but I haven't decided yet."

"Maybe we could go together. I mean, think about it. I hate solo gigs, and Boston's only a puddle jump to Stowe. The snow cover is great up there now. Ever tried snowboarding?"

Lillian laughed. "No, and I just had a vision of me tumbling down the side of a mountain face first."

"No way. I can tell you're in great shape. Boarding is awesome. Have you ever skied?"

"Sure. I learned when I was three years old."

"Then you'll be a natural. No sweat."

"Yeah, freezing my butt off probably."

"Beautiful scenery viewed from a hot tub."

"Now that's an enticing offer."

Adam kissed the side of her face. "I can see me watching your beautiful butt when both of us sail down the slope with ease. Come on—meet me in Boston for the fundraiser—come with me to Stowe."

"Maybe I will," Lillian said, "but let's take it slower. You may not want to be with me in two weeks."

"Then take me home."

"Take you home?"

"Yes. I can't go back to the hotel until the crowds clear."

Leaning into him, Lillian whispered in his ear, "What a great consolation prize!"

"I'm a consolation prize for that man who was rude to you and left?"

"No silly, for not being able to get a ticket to the concert."

He smiled. "I'll serenade you," he whispered in her ear, heating her nether regions.

"Your Irish coffee hasn't come."

"We can have a nightcap at your place."

"That sounds intimately appealing."

"I'm glad you think so."

Lillian left the restaurant to get her car, as Adam intercepted the waiter. She'd pick him up in front of the restaurant. Too many fans remained on the streets for Adam to accompany her. Where they would go and for how long—didn't matter. She'd put one foot in front of the other and move forward. Her love for Jeremy and their life together were cherished memories. But Adam Dresher, possibly another treasure, was here for her now, and he hadn't asked her age.

STRIP TEASE

JANEL GRADOWSKI

"Hi, Greg. It's Gina. I'm going to be a little late."
"Really? What a surprise." The hissing and voice distortion from the bad phone connection made her boss sound demonic. She imagined him sitting at his desk with shiny, black horns protruding from his bald spot. "What's your excuse this time? Did you break a nail or is it another bad hair day?"

Gina smiled at the steering wheel, hoping the faked gesture would infuse some cheer into her voice. "Just stuck in traffic. See you soon. Bye!"

Gina was late getting to work because of a traffic jam and missed an important meeting. A chain-reaction pile up of emergencies that needed to be solved simultaneously wreaked havoc on her carefully planned schedule.

After a day that would have made a torturer squeal with glee, she could have jogged home quicker than it took to drive. To top it all off, her car's air conditioning was on life support, only burping random blasts of lukewarm air out of the vents. She decided to call Jason to help pass the time as she crawled down the freeway.

"Help! I'm melting."

"What's the matter? Did someone dump water on my little wicked witch?" Jason's soft chuckle made Gina shiver despite the oven-like temperature in the car.

"I wish." Gina pushed her sweaty bangs off her forehead. "This stupid car is making me feel like the witch Hansel and Gretel threw in the oven."

"Poor baby."

Gina slammed on her brakes and swerved to the right, barely missing the back bumper of a Mercedes. Was there a hint of sarcasm in Jason's luscious baritone? She pounded her fist on the dash, annoyed at herself for being so stupid, on two counts. First, she nearly smashed into a car that probably cost more than her house by fantasizing about her sexy boyfriend instead of paying attention to traffic. Then she insulted Jason. She was whining about a broken air conditioner when he routinely walked into burning buildings dressed in sweltering protective gear.

"I just pulled into my driveway." It was a lie, but she needed to hang up before she dug herself into a giant hole of shame. "I'll talk to you soon."

Gina tossed her keys on the kitchen counter and dropped her purse on the table. The only thing she wanted was a nice, long shower. She poured a glass of white wine and held it to her forehead. The glass was deliciously cold as she slid it to a new position, trying to cool her overworked brain, wondering if steam was coming out of her ears.

The absolute silence in the house helped soothe the headache hammering the top of her head, attempting to crack her skull in half. There were no packs of ravenous teenagers tearing the kitchen apart looking for snacks. No slobbering dogs dancing around her legs begging to be let outside or walked. No TVs in the den, volume cranked up to the deafening level, vibrating with the chatter of hyper race announcers and thirty roaring race cars. The house was quiet, except for the hum of the refrigerator toiling away to keep its contents chilled. Champagne, brie, and Greek yogurt had replaced the old standard staples of energy drinks, pudding cups, and plastic wrapped cheese slices the kids always demanded.

Many of Gina's friends had moaned about becoming empty nesters as their youngest children approached high school graduation. They cried, thrashed and looked like lost puppies when their kids moved out and embarked on their own lives. Those women didn't know what to do when there weren't at least half a dozen people crammed around the dinner table every night.

"My baby is leaving," her best friend, Laura, had wailed, "I just don't know what I'm going to do. The only things I'm good at are being a mom and shopping."

"Is that why I haven't seen George lately? Has he been working overtime to fund your future shopping sprees?"

Other women thrived on the logistical nightmare of keeping track of the extra-curricular sports and social agendas of their children. Gina had been proficient at being the uber-mom. She juggled a part-time job, her workaholic husband's frequent business trips, and the twins' various activities like art clubs, soccer practices, and exam cram sleepovers. Nothing was forgotten or overlooked, except for Gina's cravings for privacy.

A month after Vanessa and Brandon packed up and moved across the country to start college, Harry declared he wanted a divorce and walked out. He upgraded to the firmer, perkier wife package. Or so he thought at the time.

"I'm sorry, my dear, but we've just grown apart." Harry paced around the living room like a caged tiger. "Let's just cut our losses and make a fresh start."

Gina picked up a solid glass paperweight. When Brandon was little she always made time to play catch with him. She figured her aim was probably still pretty good. When Harry was stupid enough to turn his back, she wound up and let it fly. The glass shattered on the wall beside his head. He squealed like the true pig he had turned into.

"You're crazy!"

"No, honey," Gina flashed a sweet smile, "I'm just making a fresh start. I never did like that ugly paperweight."

His swimsuit model trophy wife was now pregnant. Her ditzy, Harry liked to use the term "bubbly," personality had been stomped out by hormone fueled outbursts that could only be soothed with massive quantities of brownies, banana splits, and lasagna from the most expensive restaurants in town. It would likely take years for her to lose all of the excess weight she had packed on. Perhaps she would decide she liked the more robust version of herself and would declare that she was happily Rubenesque.

A few days earlier Gina ran into him at the grocery store. A bottle of Irish whiskey and a frozen dinner were the only things in his basket. She got in line behind him.

"Fancy meeting you here." Gina tossed a box of condoms onto the conveyor belt next to the jug of Bloody Mary mix and a can of whipped cream. "You look tired."

"Lisa wakes me up every two hours because she has to pee."

Gina pretended to study the breath mint selection. "So, where is your lovely wife?"

"Buying some kind of high-tech baby monitor." He ran his fingers through his hair, which had turned completely gray. "Apparently it's all the rage in Hollywood."

Gina studied Harry as he paid the cashier. He didn't look like the sophisticated businessman who had left her. Deep creases and wrinkles turned his face into a topographical map. The baby hadn't even arrived, but he already sported the haggard, wiped-out new parent look.

While Gina would continue to luxuriate in peaceful nights, Harry would soon be tormented with the squalling of a hungry newborn at 4 a.m. broadcast directly to his bedside by the expensive monitoring system his new wife had insisted on buying.

The divorce had been painful, but Gina knew she had come out the winner. She moved out of the six-bedroom Gothic monstrosity and into an adorable cottage with white, gingerbread trim and only one bedroom. She also found herself a smoking hot new guy, Jason. All of those decades of exercise and dieting so she could look good on Harry's arm at snobby cocktail parties had paid off. She had a closet full of little black dresses and could still turn heads, even one of a hunk who was fifteen years her junior.

Her mind wandered to the previous Friday when she attempted a sexy striptease routine after dinner. It had been a night to remember. Jason told her he loved her. On the other hand, the tablecloth from Grandma Cleo was ruined when a bottle of Chianti tipped over during the lap dance portion of the evening.

"This is a little move I like to call The Hula Shimmy Shake."

Gina held her arms out and gyrated her hips. The arm movements mimicked a baby bird trying to fly more than a graceful hula dancer. Her hips twisted and jerked as if she were trying to get an imaginary hula hoop spinning—and not succeeding.

"Come here my gorgeous Hula Girl," Jason beckoned with a crooked finger, "I love you."

Gina's movements spiraled from awkward to frenzied at Jason's proclamation. Her thigh slammed into the table. A scarlet river of wine forged a path across the middle of the white, linen tablecloth. The liquid soaked into the hand-embroidered monogram in the corner before splashing onto the floor.

"I'll get some paper towels." Jason sprinted to the kitchen. "Do you have any club soda? We can try to get the stain out."

"Don't worry about it." Gina stared at the entwined initials in the monogram—*H* and *G*. "This tablecloth isn't worth saving."

While it was easy to attract attention during happy hour at the bar, Gina was rusty at seduction. Harry had paraded her around at parties like a prize peacock, covered in sequins and jewels, but as soon as they were alone he lost interest. He would crawl into bed and start snoring within minutes. It didn't matter what she wore at night. A flannel nightgown, the sexy lingerie he often bought for her, or nothing at all—he responded with the same uninterested snorts and grunts.

Gina walked into the bedroom. The sun that had cooked her on the commute home was setting and gray shadows mottled the carpet and walls. She flipped the light on and sat her glass on the nightstand. She was anxious to lose the layers of sticky, sweaty clothing and decided to use the time to practice her strip-tease skills to ensure she wouldn't look like a clumsy oaf again.

Slowly she unbuttoned her shirt, eased it off her shoulders and tried to toss it on the bed with an elegant sweep of her arm. It caught on her wrist and snapped like a wet towel in a movie scene shot in a men's locker room. She unzipped the tight, black skirt and shimmied her hips like a belly dancer, hoping it would gracefully slide to the floor. Instead, it hung up on her thighs. A few spastic shakes later, the skirt landed in a sloppy heap around her ankles. Bra and panties came next. Both were sling-shot toward the laundry hamper. The bra ended up on the lamp-shade and the lacy panties dangled from the headboard. Gina picked up the wine glass and sashayed into the bathroom, pre-tending she was a burlesque dancer prancing off stage. She tripped on a slipper, barely catching her balance by grabbing the bathroom vanity. The fragile, crystal glass clattered into the sink and exploded into a glittering mosaic.

The phone started ringing as Gina adjusted the water temperature. She decided to let the answering machine do its job and stepped into the warm spray of water. It felt like the exhausting, exasperating day was rinsing down the drain along with the soapsuds. She imagined tiny stress monsters that looked like miniscule clones of Harry, clinging to the iridescent bubbles as they spiraled to their demise.

A siren interrupted her daydream. The sound got progres-sively louder until it made the shower tiles vibrate. It seemed to have taken up residence in front of the house.

Gina stuck her head out from behind the shower curtain, listening for the doorbell. A few weeks ago she told Jason about her fantasy of being rescued by a hunky fireman, then giving him a special thank you for saving her life.

"Hello, ma'am. Do you need some assistance?"

"Save me!"

"It's okay. You're safe now."

"Thank you, Mr. Fireman. How can I ever repay you?"

"I'm sure you can think of something."

Jason was a volunteer firefighter and his pickup was equipped with an emergency siren. Who would know if he was heading to a real fire or the one sizzling in her? Maybe he wanted to indulge in some fantasy role-playing games for the evening. The siren stopped, but no one came to the door. Gina ducked back into the shower and rinsed conditioner out of her hair.

She finished her shower and dried off with a thick towel. It felt so good to be out of her clingy clothes. She didn't bother to put on a robe.

The blinking light on the answering machine greeted her from its perch on the dresser. She stared out the window as she crossed the room. An ambulance and fire truck were parked outside, in front of the nursing home across the street. A fireman and nurse stood on the sidewalk. The nurse gestured wildly, as if she were playing an intense game of charades. The fireman was about Jason's height, but his back was turned toward her and a helmet obscured his hair.

Two paramedics exited the building pushing an old man on a gurney. The nurse stopped waving her arms around and pointed at Gina's house. Everyone turned in the direction she was pointing. The old man raised his head, smiled, and waggled his fingers at Gina when he caught sight of her through the window.

Gina screamed. She dropped to the floor and frantically rolled toward the safety of the windowless bathroom. The maneuver brought back memories of safety lessons in elementary school. You were supposed to stop, drop, and roll if you caught on fire. Between the scorching embarrassment and friction burns from the carpet, it felt like she was in an inferno.

Gina sprawled on the cool tile floor of the bathroom, trying to catch her breath. Her unused bathrobe on the door towered above her like an overbearing teacher chastising her for not thinking before she acted. When she moved in two months ago, heavy, velvet curtains covered the bedroom window. Now she knew why. Unfortunately, the curtains had been donated to charity long ago, and she never got around to buying new ones.

The phone started ringing again. Gina sighed and wondered if the nursing home could sue her for attempted murder. She closed her eyes and waited for the machine to take the message. It beeped, then Jason's voice filled the room. "Hey, Gina, it's Jason. I just wanted to say thanks for the unexpected peep show and sending some work my way, but my job is pretty secure. No need to drum up any more business for me. I'll see you tomorrow night. Maybe we can go buy some curtains for your bedroom window before dinner."

MY ONLY CONCERN

HARRIETT FORD

"Falling in love is easy. It's staying in love that's the hard part," said Amanda taking a dainty bite of her pear salad.

She looked at me across the Spring Creek Tea Room table, and added. "If you really think you can keep this younger guy interested, you might be headed for happily-ever-after land. Or you may just have the happiest three weeks of your life."

I shook my head. "No, I don't want a temporary thrill."

She fished a notepad out of her purse. "Okay, let's look at my checklist, but let me warn you. I'm an advice columnist. Not a psychologist. I don't make any guarantees."

Amanda and her checklists. She has one for every situation. And she's usually right on. I've learned to trust her advice over the years.

"That's what worries me," I said. "The staying in love part. Yes, he's very interested at the moment. But what if he finds out I wear bifocals and love to watch re-runs of *I Love Lucy* in my flannel pajamas? What if we get stuck in traffic, and I've had two cups of coffee, prunes, and a bran muffin? He may think I'm his grandmother for Pete's sake. And who the Sam Hillary is Pete anyway? An advice columnist ought to know." I teased, using a mock-quarrelsome tone.

"Pete? Pete is for *petrified*, which is what you're not. You have this age mentality holding you back, Sharon. Look at you. You're hardly Whistler's Mother. You could use a little delusion of grandeur to help you feel better about yourself."

With a conciliatory nod, I groaned, "I know I'm not exactly a total slouch. I just think he's way too young for me. He could have his pick of a dozen younger women."

"So you think he's just after one thing? Your money?"

"At my age, that's what 'one thing' usually means, unlike when we were teenagers." I rolled my eyes. "I sense that Randall is real. I mean he's genuine. It's common knowledge in Ozark that my husband left me well off when he died. Every money-hungry bachelor in the community has given me the eye. I truly don't think Randall Townsend the Third is in that category. Cheese and crackers! The man has his own plane already. But what if I'm too overwhelmed by the attention of an attractive man to see past the roses he keeps putting in front of my eyes? That's a delusion that could be dangerous." I stopped babbling to swallow a sip of tea.

"Honey, you've lived long enough to know what's real and what isn't. And speaking of real, you're not competing with women wearing implants and collagen-plumped lips." Amanda wagged a manicured, coral-nailed finger at me. "He's got to appreciate that you have a fantastic shape for a woman of any age. Why, you don't even work out at the gym."

"Yeah right. I never retain water. Just pizza and cheesecake."

"Cheesecake is the destiny that shapes my end." Amanda chuckled and patted her ample hip. She tossed her head as if she had Lauren Bacall hair hanging in shiny lengths instead of whitish, dandelion frizz.

"So tell me more about this Randall guy. Does he pay for dinner or is he saving for a rainy century?"

Knowing Amanda had once paid for several dinner-dates with a notorious moocher, I couldn't help smiling. She sometimes forgot her own advice. "Randall loves to spend money on me."

"I see. Is he one of those self-made men who worships his creator?"

"He worships God."

She gave a nod of approval. "How about wandering eyes? Does he regard every female as a passing fanny?"

I sat the glass of tea down and swallowed. "Honestly, doesn't every woman wonder about the way a guy looks at fannies? So far, I don't see any of the usual red flags."

Amanda's eyes narrowed. "You say he's divorced because his ex-wife left him for another . . . *woman*? Are you certain he's not someone who suffers from mannish depression and delusion of gender?"

"Huh?" It took a moment to digest her words. "Oh, you mean a transvestite. No. Nothing trans-gendered about this man. He's all male, shaving cream, blue denims, and boots. In fact, he could be the next Marlboro man, only he doesn't smoke, thank goodness."

"Good. No smoking. Let's see, does he drink to special occasions like the refrigerator is still running or the daily newspaper arrived?"

I chuckled, "He sometimes orders a glass of wine with dinner, but never more than one."

She made another check on her list. "Is his cholesterol number high enough that he can get into Yale?"

"He's healthy."

"Healthy enough to take you out dancing? You always enjoyed dancing."

I couldn't help giggling. "I'll follow your advice on that one."

She arched an eyebrow. "What advice?"

"You know. The easiest way to get people dancing is to hold up the line for the restroom."

Amanda laughed at that one. She always laughs at her own advice. Then her eyes narrowed in a more serious expression.

"You said he has no kids, no child-support payment, and no alimony. Looks like he's too good to be true. So here's the final question. Ready?

"What's his number?" Amanda teased, before putting her notepad back on the table. "Honestly, Sharon, just how much younger is he? Because you know, at our age, the next five years or so are going to make a huge difference in the way a woman looks. And that could be a little problem . . . or a big one. A guy doesn't get married to become a nursemaid."

"I know." I dropped my eyes. "I don't want to tell you."

She cocked her head to one side, reminding me of a curious cat. "Come on. Spit it out."

"He's just a *little* younger."

"As in five years? Ten? Fifteen?"

"He's actually, well, just ten months younger." I managed, knowing what her reaction would be.

"Ten months! Slap me with molasses and call me biscuit." She sat back in her chair with an I-can't-believe-you expression. "All that talk about re-runs and flannel P.J.'s. He probably wears bifocal too. In fact, poor vision and hearing loss is one of the biggest reasons many couples stay together. They don't notice the imperfections. He's perfect!"

She slapped the table. "If you don't keep him, I'm going after him myself."

In a downtown Springfield restaurant, Randall was having a serious conversation with his attorney. "I know Sharon sounds too good to be true," he said, "But this lady is different. She has her own money. She's not after mine. My only concern is that . . . well, that, maybe I'm a little too old for her."

ASHES REMAIN

SUSAN ELIZABETH THOMAS

"I have a full three days free next weekend." Jeannette paused to listen to her son, Scott, on the other end of the line and then responded, "Sure, honey! And I'll take you out to that steak house you've been raving about. We'll get the spendiest thing on the menu!" She beamed, mirroring the excitement she heard in his voice. *Who would've thought a twenty-eight year old man would still be thrilled to spend a long weekend with his mother?* A swelling of pride and love for her youngest filled her breast. Despite struggling with asthma as a child, a battle with bullies in his teen years, and the divorce of his parents three years ago, he turned out all right.

After nearly three decades of marriage, Jeannette's husband left, saying, "I need to find myself." Apparently, he had "found himself" with a new job, an expensive car, and a younger—much younger—wife. Jeannette grieved bitterly at first, but she eventually made peace with the situation and with God. Recently she had even begun working hard to try to forgive her ex and his new wife—fallout from making peace with God, of course. She learned that forgiveness is not saying, "What you did was okay; feel free to do it again." It's saying, "I relinquish my right to be angry, bitter or seek revenge. I'll let your own faults be their own punishment and recognize I have faults, too. By forgiving you, I free myself from any unhealthy control you have over my life." Of course, that is easier said than done, and there were days when the ashes of her pain seemed to catch and burn again within her. But, today was not one of those days.

Jeannette hung up the phone and turned her attention to the meal she had been preparing. Cooking for one was, perhaps, the primary area where Jeannette still struggled since the divorce. She gazed at the raw chicken breast lying on the plastic cutting board before her. *Should I pull out another one and prepare that one, too, and then have leftovers, or should I just make this one up for tonight?* Normally, Jeannette simply pulled out a frozen meal and popped it in the microwave, but lately, based on advice from a friend, she had decided to try to treat herself a little better. The problem with treating oneself right, however, was that it took time.

Jeannette sighed, thinking of the piles of receipts and bills waiting in her office. She re-wrapped the chicken in a new plastic baggie, returned it to the refrigerator and picked up her purse. *Who needs to cook when you work full time and there's a new bistro in town?*

"What was I thinking?" Jeannette muttered under her breath twenty minutes later. *I should've known a place like this would be crowded!* It was an unusually warm, sunny day in April, and Jeannette stood in a line teeming with "artistic" people (yet to be introduced to the novelty of deodorant) that looked like it reached from her hometown in Idaho all the way to New Jersey. *I should just give it up*, she thought, but she had already waited fifteen minutes and hated to admit defeat now that twenty people stood behind her. *Besides, this place is going to stay crowded for the next three months, and waiting that long for a shorter line seems counter-productive.*

A shade closer to her own mortality later, Jeannette found a tiny table in the corner next to an over-sized houseplant and took a seat. Upon sitting, several plant fronds landed right across her mouth and nose. She shifted her chair away. It was rather noisy in the narrow dining area, but she didn't mind. She was starving, and the tortellini soup and marinated chicken Panini before her looked amazing!

Jeannette picked up the sandwich, appreciating the sight and smell of the melting Muenster, the sprinkled herbs, and the crisp lettuce and tomatoes. She closed her eyes and opened her mouth.

"Excuse me," a voice disturbed her perfect moment.

She opened her eyes, but forgot to close her mouth a moment longer than a more sophisticated woman might. Before her stood a dark-haired young man holding a plate and a glistening glass of what looked like cola. He wore dark washed jeans and a white collared shirt, open a few buttons. He stood towering over her, smiling and looking not unlike a hopeful stray puppy. Perhaps most surprising, though, was that, despite his black hair, he had startlingly blue eyes.

"I hate to bother you, but I noticed you were sitting by yourself, and the only open spot in the restaurant is at your table. Would you mind if I join you?"

Jeannette gave her consent and the young man wasted no time plopping down beside her. She tried moving away to a more comfortable distance from him, but only found herself lost in the houseplant again. She shifted back.

Noticing her trouble, her new tablemate chuckled. "What is this, lunch or a safari expedition?"

She smiled. "Here, I'll try to make room," he said and adjusted his chair as well, but the result still maintained a snug sitting arrangement. He seemed unbothered by it. "Wow! That looks incredible! Perhaps I should've ordered what you did."

"What did you choose?"

"I got the personal Greek pizza with chicken, artichoke hearts, feta cheese and kalamata olives."

"Yum!" she replied, vaguely wondering when the friendly banter would disintegrate into an uncomfortable silence. "I'll have to try that next time."

"Have you been here before?" he asked.

"No. I thought I'd treat myself to a new experience this evening. You?"

"No. Actually, I'm new in town. I just got a job at Washington State University as an assistant professor."

"Oh, really? What department?"

"Veterinary Medicine."

"Wow! I hear they have a very good program over there. Congratulations!"

"Thanks." The charm of his smile caught her off guard.

"So what brings you all the way into Moscow, Idaho, in the middle of the week?" She quipped. The two cities, though separated by a state line, were a mere eight miles apart.

"I was going to meet a friend over here. He cancelled at the last minute, but I decided to come anyway. My refrigerator is still empty."

"Well, I'm sorry you got stuck with me instead of getting to see your friend."

"I'm not." He smiled again and it warmed her. "He's just an acquaintance from college—not even a good friend, really, but I was desperate for company. He's the only person I know here, until now." He smiled again at her.

She returned it. "Well, it's nice to meet you . . . uh . . . uh . . ."

"Jason."

"I'm Jeannette."

"Thanks for sharing your table with me, Jeannette."

"My pleasure."

With the pleasantries and introductions over, they began to eat their meals. Still, Jason continued to chat with her comfortably. She learned his new professorship was his first job out of college, that he was unmarried, but came from a large family, and that he enjoyed a newly popular musical group she had never heard of called Ashes Remain. He was obviously a people-person and, though he was short on friends now, she had no doubt he'd be surrounded by admirers within a few weeks.

About ten minutes into their conversation, Jeannette noticed a purple stain on Jason's sleeve. To her chagrin he noticed her staring at the mark and bent his arm to examine it more closely.

"Oh, I bought some blueberries and was adding them to my cereal this morning and accidentally leaned my arm on one of them. I didn't notice it until I was already at work. Wore my jacket all day to keep it hidden. I hope I didn't ruin this shirt. It's new and one of only a few that I bought for work."

"No, you haven't ruined it. Don't wash it yet. First run boiling hot water through the stained fabric until the discoloration comes out."

"Really? That's all? Just hot water?"

"Yep. Boiling hot water. Should work just fine. That's how I always get out berry juice."

"Awesome. Thanks!"

As they finished their meal, Jeannette was actually sorry to know she would probably never run into this young man again. "Well, I'm glad you decided to join me. It was nice talking to you and much better than eating alone."

Jason smiled that brilliant smile. "It was my pleasure. Uh, forgive me, but I noticed you aren't wearing a wedding ring, and I wonder if you might not mind sharing another meal sometime."

Jeannette was taken fully by surprise. Jason seemed like a stable, intelligent, easy-going, kind young man and he was certainly good looking, but it had never crossed her mind that he might have enjoyed her company enough to seek it again. For one thing, he was easily twenty years her junior. Throughout the meal, she assumed he was just making the best of a bad situation, what with the seating being so limited. But now, looking in his blue eyes, she saw a genuineness to his request. It had been a long time since she had seen true attraction in the eyes of a man, but she recognized it when it was there. It was there.

"Ummm . . . I, uh . . ." she cleared her throat and started over. "I, uh, I'm divorced, actually." That was not an answer to his question, she realized, but that was what came out.

"Well, if you're available, I'd love to treat you sometime. Say, next Friday night?"

"You are a very nice young man, but . . ."

"And you're a very nice young woman."

Young? She thought, and then prayed, *Lord, is he blind? What do I do?*

"Look, I know there's a difference in our ages, but I like you. You're fun, attractive, interesting . . . I think we would have fun together."

Did he say "attractive"? Jeannette hadn't thought of herself as attractive in a long time. Even before her marriage ended she had stopped feeling desirable as a woman. Lately, of course, she had started taking better care of herself. She had colored her hair, gotten some exercise and was now a comfortable size eight. Nothing could change the fact that she was aging, but she felt good, looked good, and was beginning to enjoy facing life on more positive terms.

"Well, I'll be out of town all weekend," she said. She almost added, "with my son," but didn't.

"Are you free Monday night? Or are weekdays bad?"

"Monday is okay," she answered, still treading cautiously.

"Can I get your number?"

Jeannette fumbled in her purse for a pen, wondering if she might come across her missing brain in there, too. *What am I thinking?* But Jason wasn't exactly a child. He was younger than she, to be sure, but he was a grown man with a paying job. He was probably in his thirties—or very nearly so—and he had a comfortable manner about him. Furthermore, he didn't come across like a pervert or a drunk. He hadn't made a single sexual innuendo and had ordered a Pepsi—two things which made him stand out. In her experience, if men of his age weren't thinking of sex, they were thinking of beer, or vice versa. What men don't seem to know is that both topics are turn-offs to women. A woman wants a man who thinks of *her*—not just of her drunk and naked.

Jeannette found the pen. *Why shouldn't I go out with him? Older men go out with younger women all the time. My husband sure did.* There is was again—that little twinge of bitterness. She swallowed it back and scribbled her number on a napkin.

On Friday, Jeannette made the six-hour drive to Seattle. Scott greeted her with a hug and soon they were seated together in a cozy two-person booth at his favorite steakhouse.

"How's the new job?" she asked.

"It's okay, but I don't really know anybody there yet. I don't know if it's going to work out here."

"What do you mean?"

"I don't know . . . I was thinking I might move back to Moscow and see if I can't get a job nearer to home."

"It's not working out with Jen, is it?"

"No. She dumped me."

"I thought you had only gone on a few dates. Don't you have to be boyfriend and girlfriend for somebody to 'dump' you?"

"Well, then she pre-dumped me. I don't know. I just know we're not going to go out anymore."

"Sorry."

"Really?"

"No, not really. I thought she was a bit worldly for you." The girl cared for nothing but jewelry, shoes, and the latest fashions. Jeannette, for one, was thrilled to hear they'd called it quits.

"Yeah, probably." Scott sounded mildly depressed, but she knew it was more from just feeling lonely and homesick than from actually losing Jen. Jeannette had no intention of allowing him to move home again. She loved him, but he needed to learn to make it on his own. He was twenty-eight and no longer needed a mother—at least, not full time.

"Maybe you should just put your resumé out there and see what else comes up," she suggested. "Who knows, maybe you'll get a job in Hawaii or New Mexico or Virginia or somewhere interesting. You've always said you wanted to see more of the country."

"Maybe."

Their steaks came, sizzling and smelling amazing, alongside heaps of herb and garlic mashed potatoes and steamed vegetables.

"Here's one for you," the waiter said, "and one for your mother."

Funny, Jeannette thought, *no one told* him *I was Scott's mother. I guess it's obvious. Oh, well.*

They prayed and plowed in.

"I'm starving!" Scott said around a mouthful of the juicy, medium rare steak. "There's nothing to eat at my house."

"Why not? Don't you go shopping?"

"Sort-of. Mostly I just don't cook and I ran out of frozen dinners three days ago."

"Good grief! You can *read,* can't you? What happened to that cookbook I got you for Christmas?"

"I'm using it." He chewed and swallowed. "It's propping up the leg of my futon."

Jeannette rolled her eyes.

"Oh, Mom, do you know how to get soy sauce stains out? I went to a Chinese fast food place in the mall with some friends last Friday and sat on one of those soy sauce packets. I got a big black stain all over the seat of my favorite jeans! It was embarrassing!"

Jeannette couldn't help snickering.

"It's not funny, Mom! I was riding with them, so I couldn't go home and change. I had to tie my hoody around my waist like some teenage girl to hide my butt. It made me fit in a *little too well* with the Seattle men, if you know what I mean."

Jeannette was laughing shamelessly now.

"Stop laughing! The clerk at Old Navy winked at me! It was a *guy!*"

Tears now streamed freely down her face and her sides hurt. "Well, you *are* awfully cute!" she managed through lungs constricted with laughter.

"Thanks a lot, Mom!" he sulked. "Now the stain is on my hoody, too."

Despite his annoyance, Scott was not immune to the contagious mirth of his mother. Seeing her doubled over and barely able to breathe from the laughter, caused him to also recognize the hilarity. A few minutes later, they were still chuckling.

"So, are you going to help me get the stain out, or not?" He finally asked through a large grin, passing her a napkin with which to wipe her eyes.

"Oh, sorry, son," she gasped, trying to calm herself. "Try running cold water through the back of the stain. Then get what's left out with dish detergent. You may have to work it in and scrub it for a while."

"Can you do it for me?"

"What? Scott, you're a grown man!"

"Please?"

"Oh, all right. Show them to me when we get back to your apartment. And I hope you changed the sheets on your bed, because that's where I'm sleeping. You can have the couch."

Scott grinned.

As the evening continued, a strange sensation began to settle on Jeannette. Something seemed just a little off. She was having a wonderful time with her son, of course. However, there was a thought growing in the back of her mind that she kept pushing back. It wasn't until they were in the car going home that it came blazing to the forefront of her mind.

"What is this music you have playing, Scott?"

"Oh, that's my new favorite group. They're called Ashes Remain. Cool, huh? Ever heard of them?"

Jeannette paused. "Uh, yes, actually. Yes, I have."

Usually, when driving home from Seattle, Jeannette was anxious to get home, quickly tiring of the long, winding roads. This time she was thankful for the solitary hours. She had a lot on her mind. It was Sunday evening and Jason said he would be calling either tonight or sometime on Monday. She had to decide what she would say when—if—he did.

Jeannette popped her son's borrowed Ashes Remain CD in and listened, trying to just hear the music—hear what Jason and Scott heard—hear *herself*. Four songs later she stopped the CD. She knew what she was going to say.

Riiiiinnnng! Caller ID told her it was Jason. Her answer interrupted the third ring. "Hello? Yes, of course, I remember.

Yes, well, actually, I'm not going to be able to make it. No, no, it's just that, well, I don't think we have much in common—at least, not enough for me. You see, Jason, I'm a grown woman with a grown son. You're a lot like him, to tell the truth. But that's just the problem. If you and I went out, I would feel more like your mother than like your date. And I'd look like it, too, I'm afraid."

She listened to Jason's protests, and it was nice to hear his compliments again. He claimed he just saw her for who she was and she believed him. Still, Jeannette stood her ground. She finally knew what she wanted, although it took young, handsome, sweet Jason to help her figure it out—to put together the pieces of the remainder of her pain and what she had learned about herself from it. She finally knew what she wanted. She wanted a man who liked the same things she liked, whose *home* was wherever he lived, and who wouldn't starve or go naked if there wasn't a woman in his life to cook for him and do his laundry. She wanted a man who was a *man*—fully grown, physically and emotionally. She wanted a man who knew *who* he was and knew *where* he was. And she *deserved* such a man. She had earned it.

MY LIVE-IN LANGUAGE LAB

KARIN L. FRANK

My name is Margaret, Maggie. I work as a cocktail waitress in Betty's Bar and Grill, an establishment in the local arts district. There I'm known mostly by my nickname— Melons. The obvious reasons for this nickname have ripened over the years, but they haven't developed dimples, brown spots or rot.

I never had the chance to finish college, but I still read a great deal. And somewhere in my middle years, I got the hankering to learn a foreign language. So for my fifty-fifth birthday, I treated myself to French classes at the local Junior College.

I ran into trouble right off the bat.

"You're not paying attention," the young professor said. She peered down from the Olympian heights of her greater knowledge and shook her well-kempt head of hair at me. "Maybe you don't really want to be in this class."

She was right about the first part but not about the second.

French was scheduled from 8 a.m. to 10 a.m. five days a week. So every morning, except Monday, I was coming to class on four hours sleep.

"I want to," I replied and tried by my expression to get the rest of the story across to her. With the usual economy of language that tired cocktail waitresses learn to use, I lifted an eyebrow and shrugged a shoulder. Normally that works, but it didn't with her.

She huffed, said something in French that sounded derogatory and stalked back to the front of the room.

I was crushed.

But the situation didn't improve.

The boredom factor reared its sluggish head.

In addition to the classroom time, we had to put in a certain number of hours in the language lab. But language lab, unfortunately, was far more sterile than class. After all, you're talking to a computer. And a computer is answering you back. Until the day that androids walk the earth, computers are going to produce the ultimate in dull conversation.

I fell asleep more than once.

Talking in class was fun. Even though I was making a fool of myself most of the time, I enjoyed trying to imitate French pronunciation. So many English words, I found, had actually once been French. But the French had this, to my mind, delightfully twisted way of pronouncing them. And I loved how my nose always felt as though I needed to sneeze by the time class had ended.

I started peppering my barroom jargon with French words. "We try our best to maintain the most congenial milieu," I told the 6 p.m. crowd who come in to wind down with a cool one before braving the train for home. That bunch can always use a laugh. They'd look startled for a moment, then my exaggeratedly nasal delivery of the word *milieu* hit them and they roared.

After several months, during which I did manage to master some basic grammar, I quit. After all, this had been a gift to myself, not a punishment.

But a new path to learning French opened before me.

I was given the chance to obtain the services of a *sleeping dictionary*. The sleeping kind is not as easy to procure as the book kind.

Young ladies today actively seek romance and sex. I'm the kind of woman who likes to indulge her tastes with whatever falls onto her path.

Guilluame was such a windfall. He came into the bar looking for a job. Guilluame was a foreign exchange student. He spoke French, his native language, fluently and English hesitantly. His body language spoke volumes. What more could any student of language ask of a dictionary.

"A job?" Betty, the eponymous owner of Betty's Bar and Grill, asked. "Doing what?"

"Any zing," he answered. "Wait zee table. Wash zee dish . . . dishes."

I looked up and down his tall, slender frame, dark boudoir eyes, and wavy brown hair. I wouldn't say I pounced on him. I'm not the pouncing kind. I'd say more that I gravitated toward those muscle masses so nicely delineated by the drape of his neat, white T-shirt.

"How old are you?" Betty asked. She's always been careful about the law.

"Twenty-two, Mademoiselle. Old enough to work in the bar."

"Old enough to know what's what?" I asked. I've always been careful about rules other than the law.

"What is what?" He paused to mull that over. Then his eye brightened and he said, "*Oui*."

My first French conversation outside of the classroom!

I cocked an eyebrow and a hip at him. "That means 'yes,' right?"

"Right, yes." His eyes twinkled.

"This is Melons," Betty introduced me.

"*Que*, Melons?" Guilluame asked, as any young man might.

This necessitated an explanation offered in hesitant French by Betty.

"Soo," Guillaume replied. He responded with a lilting sentence, delivered in an approving tone, in which the only word I caught was *derrière*.

What a charming young man, I thought.

I knew right then that he was bright enough to respond to innuendo and context as much as words. He'd make an excellent dictionary.

Of course, I couldn't just throw a rope around him and haul him home. That's kidnapping and frowned upon in our culture. I'd have to lure him. I'd have to offer him something that all those art school hotties couldn't, or I'd lose him to language lessons for younger derrieres.

"What are you doing in America," I asked him, "when you can speak French?"

"*Oui*, French," he said, smearing his delightful accent all over the two words. "I am student. I study the art at the Institute."

Now what can a middle-aged barmaid offer a hot, French art student that he can't get from others of his class and age?

"How about a place to stay?" I asked. "Are you in a dorm?"

Betty translated the gist of this.

"*Non*," Guilluame replied.

"You offering?" Betty asked with obvious amusement.

"*Oui*." I replied. "*Pourquoi pas*." I hoped I had gotten the grammar correct when I saw Betty grin.

She owns the whole building. I rent the apartment above the bar. It has a guest room with its own private bathroom. I do have friends over occasionally. But most times Betty likes me to keep that room for barroom clientele who get past a certain limit of drunkenness. She's afraid for them if they have to drive home.

She's pretty good at cutting people off, so it doesn't happen often.

But she must have seen where I was going with this, and she nodded.

So Guilluame moved in. And my French lessons began.

Since at first we only met in the tiny kitchen in the morning, we started with nouns for food and drink. Guilluame handprinted labels and tacked them up on the walls in French and English.

Cheese is *fromage* and coffee is *café*. But the simple bagel becomes *le petit pain en couronne*, a small bread in the shape of a crown. You can't get that delightful tidbit out of a computer.

We had even more fun with the verbs. On many mornings before we went downstairs to our jobs and his classes, we amused ourselves over breakfast acting out the simpler ones.

Other verbs came later.

Being an artist, Guilluame needed models. He asked if he could sketch the inanimate objects around the apartment. "Furniture," he said. "It interests me. And vases." He ran his hand over the curves of my favorite blown glass piece. "They're like the bodies of women."

"*Oui*," I replied.

"And may I sketch the apples, pears, and grapes on the table?" he asked. He pointed at each fruit as he recited their names in English.

"Oh, *Oui. Sur la table*," I replied with a grin. "*La pomme, la poire et le raisin*."

While he sketched bowls of fruit, we talked about verbs used to shop, to buy, and to eat.

Then one morning, we met in the hallway as I was exiting the bathroom. Demurely, I let slip a fold of my fluffy blue terrycloth robe.

"May I sketch?" he asked immediately, "The fruits that are not on the table?"

"Oh, *oui*," I replied. *Yes* had become one of my favorite words to say to him.

"*Au naturel?*"

"*Certainement.*"

His sketches grew more intimate and my vocabulary more elaborate. My learning rate accelerated. And after a while, in bed at night, I practiced the finer points of what he'd taught me of the French tongue.

We continued in that vein for many months. But even the most productive of exchanges must face the vicissitudes of art. Guilluame needed to return to France.

"I want to study sculpture," he advised me.

"Learning," I agreed, "is a life-long process."

I now speak fluent French, but it's too quiet in my apartment since he moved. Lately, I've been thinking that Spanish might also be an interesting language to learn. I won't waste any hours attending a class this time. I'll go straight to the learn-at-home technique.

A young Guatemalan art student has been stopping in frequently for a beer after class. He needs help expressing himself in English. But he's been sketching my melons on the cocktail napkins.

That's a good sign.

VENA'S RULES OF ENGAGEMENT

SYLVIA A. STRAUB

"What's wrong, darling? You look terribly unhappy." Ellen Murphy, my best friend since high school, had asked me to meet her for drinks at our favorite bar.

"Oh, Vena, I've been in a rut since my divorce from that louse." She drained half her cosmo. "I want to meet some men, but—."

Poor Ellen had been the last to know that her Richard had hit on every female he'd met. Including me. "But, you're not sure how to go about it."

"I guess not." Her expression said, "You don't have to rub it in."

Ellen had no idea how much I could help her. In my late forties, after the mourning period for my beloved husband David, I began developing Rules of Engagement. These rules usually referred to regulations soldiers followed in combat; mine were about attracting men. Ellen needed to start with *Rule One: Know what you want.*

"Do you just want someone to go out with, or would you like to remarry?" No one could ever replace my David, so I chose never again to tie the knot. Having a good time with a male friend that included a physical relationship suited me just fine.

"I'd like to meet some men now. I'll think about marriage later."

Good enough. Ellen was ready for *Rule Two: Don't be a working stiff; take time to enjoy life.* "Ellen, men aren't attracted to workaholics." She bristled at my comment.

"If you want to be a successful attorney, you have to work your buns off." She brushed back strings of mousy brown hair. "Besides, the managing partner wouldn't allow me to hire more people."

Baloney. Ellen needed to work smarter. "Look, you're a partner, too. Delegate to the associates. That's why they were hired." I paused to let the thought sink in.

"You're right." She nodded. "I've been racking up billable hours, and I haven't taken time for myself."

It showed in her appearance. "Come to my party next Friday. You'll meet several attractive, somewhat younger, men." *Rule Three: Be open to relationships with younger guys.*

"You've gotta be kidding." Ellen's frown revealed deep lines in her forehead. "I'm not about to rob the cradle."

I leaned forward. "My dear friend, in DC, the number of available men our age is small, unless you count the divorced ones and the workaholics." She didn't need either of those types right now. "Younger, unmarried men have active social lives, and most are open to meeting mature women."

Ellen rolled her violet eyes. "Okay, I'm game."

"Good." After hitting her hard with Rule Three, I thought it best to ease her into *Rule Four: Always look your best.* Ellen's gray roots were a disgrace, and she hadn't had her clothes altered, or bought new ones, since she'd lost weight. "Tomorrow, we'll shop for a new dress for you to wear at the party. Then, we'll luxuriate at my spa."

I assumed Ellen would offer to pay me back for my time and effort after she connected with a man. I'd ask her to handle a lawsuit I planned to file. A client had defaulted on payment for services rendered by my public relations company.

"I could sure use a break." She took a deep breath, as if relieved to be on the way out of her rut. "Are you still dating that cute guy who works for a senator?"

"Oh, Lloyd." I grimaced. "He's so wrapped up in himself, I lost interest." *Rule Five: Have relationships only with men you enjoy being around.*

"Who are you going out with now?"

Ellen must have assumed that I was never without a man. Guilty. My PR firm put me in touch with lots of guys. "A physic professor at George Washington University. Brett McAllister. I met him at the press conference I organized to launch his new book on climate change. We clicked imme-diately. He's intelligent and charming. In his late thirties." I didn't tell her that our relationship had just begun.

Ellen smiled. "I'm dying to meet him."

Red alert. Would my best friend make a play for Brett? Surely she wasn't that desperate. I dismissed the thought.

The next morning, I picked Ellen up at her condo, and we headed for Chevy Chase. After checking out dresses at Neiman-Marcus, Lord & Taylor, and Bloomingdales, we found a violet silk sheath that showed off Ellen's figure and highlighted her eyes. I felt a bit jealous that she wore a size six, whereas I struggled to fit into a size ten. But I had curves, and Ellen's body was straight as a railroad tie.

Off we went to the spa. Everything was pink—walls, tables, chairs, uniforms, and towels. With romantic music wafting through the air, we enjoyed a rock massage. So soothing. Ellen's facial muscles had relaxed, and she looked more rested. While I had a manicure and a pedicure, a stylist colored Ellen's hair a rich brown with caramel highlights and gave her a layered cut. My dear friend looked ten years younger. Next, the spa's top makeup artist worked on both of us, bringing out our best features.

When he had finished, I went over to Ellen. "You look exquisite, darling. The makeup emphasizes your gorgeous eyes." And hid her ugly frown lines.

Ellen swiveled in her chair, grabbed a hand mirror, and gazed at herself—forever it seemed—before smiling her approval. "Vena, what you and the wonderful people here have done for me today has given me confidence to get back into circulation." She put the mirror on her lap, held out her arms, and we hugged.

"How can I ever repay you?"

Little did she know. "Don't worry about that now."

Ellen was on her way to fulfilling *Rule Four: Always look your best*. Though she still had a long way to go.

The day of the party, I stayed home to check last-minute details. Reviewing the invitation list, I felt pleased with my mix of guests—friends, clients, and my wonderful staff. By inviting Lloyd, I'd invoked *Rule Six: Keep in touch with former beaux; they might have fascinating male friends*. I was relieved that he'd be out of town that weekend. Several of the single men on my list had RSVP'd that they weren't bringing dates. I felt sure Ellen would hit it off with one of them.

I donned my new red satin gown and checked myself out in the full-length mirror. The color complemented my chestnut hair, and the style was slimming. I had some champagne before the florist delivered the arrangements and the caterer brought the hors d'oeuvres. The waiter came and set up the bar. When the musician showed up, she practiced softly on my grand piano.

Ellen was the first guest to arrive. The waiter took her wrap and brought her a flute of champagne. I told her about several men I wanted her to meet. "You'll enjoy them."

Ellen smiled and nodded. "I'm sure I will." She stared at me. "You look spectacular in that red gown, Vena."

"Thank you, my dear, beautiful friend." I hugged her. When we had first started going out with boys in high school, we'd often exchange compliments to bolster each other's confidence.

The doorbell rang, and I excused myself. After greeting my guests, I introduced them to Ellen. One of the single men struck up a conversation with her. As more people arrived, I circulated, wondering if Brett would ever show up.

He was the last guest to appear. I had wanted people to know that we were a couple, but he apparently had other ideas. Coming to the party late was a slap in the face, given what I'd done for him.

Brett kissed me on the cheek. "You look lovely, my dear." He glanced around as he spoke. "You sure know how to throw a great party."

"Well, I've had some experience organizing events." Had he forgotten the press conference that had put his book on best-seller lists around the country?

With the heel of his palm, he slapped his forehead. "Oh, of course. And you really are superb at what you do."

I caught a hint of contempt in his voice, as if he'd put me in the same category as a cashier at a car wash. "Darling, I'd like you to meet some of my friends."

"Oh, sweetheart, I need to use the little boys' rooms first." He whimpered like a child who'd pee in his pants if he didn't get to the bathroom in time. No doubt he wanted to scan the crowd by himself.

"You know where it is." I waved my hand toward the powder room.

Moments later, a client tapped me on the shoulder and asked if we could talk in private.

I had invited Tom Hammond to my party because I wanted to get to know him better. In his early forties, he was soft spoken and courteous, not to mention handsome and well dressed.

"Let's talk in my library."

I led him there, and we sat down in front of the fireplace.

"Vena, as you know, my company will soon launch a new men's sportswear line, and I had hoped you would design the promotion plan."

I could tell that he didn't want me to delegate it to my staff. "Tom, I'd be delighted to. Why don't we set up a time to discuss a strategy?"

He smiled as if he'd won the lottery. "Could we do lunch at Beauvilliers sometime next week?"

I almost fainted. Beauvilliers was the most elegant and expensive restaurant in the city. I had been there only once and looked forward to going again. "I would love to. Tuesday is a good day for me."

"Done. I'll have someone phone you about a convenient time and send a car to pick you up."

If Tom had wanted to make an impression, he'd succeeded. "How kind of you." I wondered if he'd send a limo or a Lincoln Continental. Either would be fine.

We chatted for a few moments more, then he apologized for leaving the party early to catch a plane.

I returned to the great room in a trance, but my euphoria evaporated when I spotted Brett and Ellen alone on the chilly balcony, laughing. What were they doing out there? As I was about to join them, I caught Brett staring down the neckline on Ellen's dress. He wouldn't find much there.

I continued with my hostess duties. An hour later, I looked around for Brett. He and Ellen were still outside, French kissing. For a moment, I went numb, then I shut the balcony door and lowered the blind. No one spoke to me about their flagrant behavior, but I noticed several guests whispering among themselves. Others looked at each other as if offended at what they'd seen. I prayed I wouldn't lose clients because of them.

I continued circulating, chatting up my guests and laughing at their jokes. As people began to leave, I saw that the balcony door was open, and Ellen and Brett had disappeared. When everyone had gone, I collapsed onto the sofa and sobbed.

Both had humiliated me by behaving badly. After all I'd done for Ellen, I didn't know if I could ever forgive her. And given Brett's conduct that evening, I considered our relationship severed.

I felt better when I thought about my *Rule Seven: Never waste time in a bad relationship; look forward to the next one.* Could Tom be the new man in my life?

Dabbing my eyes with tissues, I realized that I hadn't told Ellen about *Rule Eight: Proceed slowly with a new man.* She'd fallen for the first guy who had paid any attention to her since her divorce and had behaved like a pitiful, love-starved spinster. What a fool she was to let Brett make a spectacle of her.

The next day, Ellen phoned. I didn't answer. She left a message of apology for her behavior and invited me for a drink after work on Monday. My only reason for accepting her offer was to make her feel guilty enough to manage my lawsuit. I'd have my secretary return her call in the morning.

When I entered our favorite haunt, Ellen was already there and had ordered two cosmos. As I approached, I saw tears spilling down her cheeks. I was not moved. She brushed them away with the back of her hand, then got up and gave me a hug. I did not hug her back.

"Vena, there aren't words to tell you how awful I feel about what happened at your party."

We sat down, and I sipped my cosmo without responding.

"Brett swept me off my feet. I hadn't been kissed by a man since I left that . . . that . . ."

"Jerk." I took another sip.

"How can I make it up to you?" Her eyes beseeched me.

I was about to broach the lawsuit, but my memories of our friendship stopped me. Ellen had been wonderfully supportive when I lost David. I had always counted on her when I needed a friend. And now, she counted on me to help her meet an attractive man. I took a deep breath.

"Let's put this Brett thing behind us. We've seen the kind of person he is, and neither of us has to settle for that . . . that . . ."

"Jerk." Ellen burst out laughing.

"Touché." I laughed because she did, and neither of us could stop.

The few people in the bar stared at us. Finally, we got hold of ourselves and raised our glasses.

"To our friendship," Ellen said.

"Friends, forever," I replied.

After we finished our drinks, we ordered another round.

As we sipped our cosmos, we chatted about Ellen's wardrobe and planned a shopping spree for the weekend. When she went to the ladies room, I gazed out the window. Suddenly a new rule occurred to me. *Rule Nine: Don't introduce your best friend to the man in your life until the relationship is well established.* Or, unless you want to break if off.

SPEED DATING

MARY ELLEN MARTIN

Jackie sipped water, surveying the room. Pathetic. Musical people instead of chairs. Musical, desperate, balding, overweight people. Jackie was thankful she didn't have to count herself in that crowd. Well, except for the desperate part.

How did Trish talk her into this? Trish hardly needed a wingman. In twenty minutes, she collected at least ten phone numbers or emails, while Jackie answered lackluster questions from people out of her league for various reasons. Jackie was dressed for the weather, not the A/C. When the goose bumps came, she laughed, telling dater number five it was the air conditioning (the only truth that night). She told number eight it was a reaction to his cologne, and by dater twelve, it was full-on malaria.

Jackie looked at Trish, laughing and confident in her jump-me dress. Despite her surgically altered assets, she had a long string of short-term relationships. She was proof there were no guarantees. Jackie sighed, resigning herself to lower standards. Way lower.

"Everyone!" called the host. "Take your places. The next round is starting. Smile and have fun!" She rang a small bell, and Jackie plastered her smile back on. Candidate thirteen sat down. His name tag said Roy. He didn't look like a Roy. Roy was an old guy who played guitar on that TV show *Hee Haw*.

This Roy obviously wouldn't know who Roy Clark was. He was too young to be speed dating, Jackie thought. He hardly looked college aged. And cute. What was he doing here?

Roy began his pitch, which Jackie had to admit wasn't bad. Good eye contact, nice smile, the minty breath barely covering the garlic. Jackie pegged him as a business major, which would make her guilty of statutory rape, if this kept up. *Please God, let him be eighteen,* she thought.

Jackie took a breath to begin her story in a minute or less, when Roy got a horror-stricken look on his face. "Uh oh." He said, turning red and fidgeting.

"What's wrong? Is there something in my teeth?" Jackie asked.

"Uh, no. You're gorgeous, really." Jackie suddenly felt tingly, until his next statement. "I had Italian earlier, and the cheese—"

The smell hit. "Oh my God!"

"I'm sorry. Uh, awkward." Roy sipped his water, wiping his brow with his arm. Jackie grabbed her napkin and held it to her face.

"No, really, it's okay. Not your fault. Just another last straw." Jackie took short breaths through her mouth and saw people at nearby tables noticing. Noses wrinkled, eyes squinted, and for all the *ignoring* they were doing, they couldn't be more obvious.

Roy stammered on. "I was nervous about coming, you know? I let a friend talk me into this, and well . . ."

Jackie grabbed her purse. "Next time, try Valium or beer. You're nice enough, but that was the deal breaker. Well, that and the fact that you don't look old enough to vote." Roy stood and reached in his inside jacket pocket.

"Wait! Please, I'm sorry. Here's my card. This is a horrible first impression, I know, but I'd like to get to know you."

Jackie took the card in politeness, promising herself to toss it later. She waved at Trish and rushed from the room, not waiting to see if her friend would follow.

That night, Jackie was at Trish's, pouring blended drinks while Trish sorted business cards on her kitchen table.

"Are you alphabetizing them?" Jackie asked, bringing the glasses over.

Trish shook her head. "Income. This group here," she waved over the row of cards on her left, "make probably forty thou a year or less."

"How can you tell?"

"It's all in the shoes and lapels. Seriously. I have an eye for this. This row in the middle, I'd say they make maybe fifty to sixty. And this group here are simply too good to be true." Trish took one of the "good" cards, and marked an *X* on it.

"What's that?" Jackie asked.

"Oh, I watched this guy. Maybe mid-fifties, handsome, but driving a rented Lexus. So he's from out of town cheating on his wife, or trying to show some fake flash to get a date. Or both. Who knows?"

Jackie frowned, sipping her daiquiri. "Wow, it's not like you to be so selective."

"I realized my current method of choosing men needed revising. You won't believe this, but I think I'll try for a happy medium between your method and mine."

"You're right. I don't buy it. And I don't have a method."

"That's what I'm saying! Come on, Jake, when are you going to realize you need a man? You cannot spend your life watching *30 Rock* and *Xena* reruns and playing computer solitaire!"

Jackie sighed. "Stop calling me that."

"Never. You get flushed when you're angry. Since you refuse makeup, I will stoop to beautify you any way possible. Really not that hard, you're a knockout already. Just a little blush and—"

"Trish . . ." Jackie warned.

"Oh, whatever. But I'm serious about you getting out there. Look me in the eye and tell me this is what you thought," she lifted her hands and made air quotes, "forty-something would be like."

Jackie leaned back, turning her glass in her hands. "Tell you the truth, I don't know what I expected. My goals never included being divorced by the time I was thirty-seven. Now . . ." Jackie shrugged and took a drink. "My sisters sent dead roses last week, and I have a stack of 'Over the Hill' cards from my coworkers. I have age spots on my body that were freckles ten years ago. And don't make fun of my TV habits. Lucy Lawless and Tina Fey are my heroes, you know that."

Trish sipped her drink and wrinkled her nose. "Good Lord, what's this?"

"Rum."

"No, no. We need tequila." Trish got up and moved her chair. She climbed up, reaching in the cabinet over the stove, and pulled out a bottle of Cuervo. "There, that's the stuff."

"Wait, there's half a blender of daiquiri left," Jackie protested.

Trish cracked the seal on the bottle. "What is this blender of which you speak?"

Two days later, the knock on the door shouldn't have made Jackie uncomfortable, but when she heard it, the hair on the back of her neck rose. She looked through the peephole.

"Oh my God!"

She opened the door to find Trish, nose bloodied and one eye swelling shut, leaning against the door frame. Jackie helped her to the couch and reached for the phone.

"No, don't," Trish protested. "No cops." Her breath rattled as she spoke.

"You don't call the shots when you get beat up. Dale would have gotten away with it if you hadn't done this for me, remember?" Jackie dialed 911 and gave the address, running—*Don't freak, don't freak, don't freak*—to get ice. After hanging up, she took a breath—*chill out, chill out, don't let her see you panic*—and faced her friend. "What happened?"

Trish winced as the ice pack touched her face. "Nothing. Tonight just didn't go as planned." She tried to smile, but it turned into a grimace of pain.

"Understatement from hell. Where else are you hurt?"

Trish licked her lips, crusty with blood. "Hard to talk."

Jackie nodded. She made sure the porch light was on, and sat next to Trish, holding the ice pack to her face. It was difficult not to gag at the mixed smells of blood and perfume.

God, Trish, were you this scared when this happened to me?

After a lifetime, the ambulance finally rolled up. She ran to the door and opened it before the EMTs had time to get their gear out. A familiar face made her groan.

"Hey, Jackie, good to see you. 'Sup?" Roy asked.

"Spare me. She's in here." Jackie showed Roy and his partner into her living room. Trish gave a weak smile.

"Well, well, fate takes a hand. Ray, right?"

"It's Roy. Jeez, what happened to you?"

Roy's partner looked back and forth between the three. "You know them?"

"Focus, people. My friend is bleeding on my couch!" Jackie shouted. Roy knelt to listen to her heart, while his partner started asking Trish where it hurt. Jackie moved to let more firefighters in the room, which quickly became crowded. Jackie pressed herself against a wall and tried to hide her discomfort.

Roy smiled up at Jackie. "You didn't return my emails. And before you ask, Trish here gave me your email address. Can I get a second chance?" Roy's partner looked stunned.

"This is the woman you farted away? You moron." The other man, who appeared to be about the same age as Roy, gave her the once over. "You said she was gorgeous, but forgot to add cradle robber."

Jackie slapped her forehead. "You told him? He's right, you are a moron." Trish whooped silent laughter and began to struggle.

"Easy now, Trish. We've got you. Relax." Roy looked at his partner and nodded at his silent question. The partner motioned to the firefighters, who left and came back with a gurney. "Can you tell us what happened?" Trish shook her head, giving a warning look at Jackie.

"Don't, Jake."

Roy looked from Trish to Jackie.

Jackie glared back at Trish. "She won't say. For all I know, a hooker was defending her turf."

Roy nodded. "I doubt there's room in the ambulance for you. Can you follow us?"

"Um, I don't drive." Jackie crossed her arms, then put them down, put her hands in her pockets, and then crossed her arms again.

Roy hung his head. His partner snorted and kept working on Trish. "Okay, you can ride up front with us, but it'll be tight." Jackie thought about pressing her body up next to Roy in the ambulance and tried to push the ensuing naughty fantasies out of her head.

"Whatever. Just help her."

"Why does Trish call you 'Jake' instead of 'Jack'?" Roy asked.

Jackie sipped her coffee and made a face. "To get my goat. She's done that since we were kids. Ugh, you weren't kidding about this coffee."

Roy chuckled. "I never said the hospital cafeteria was fine dining, but the cinnamon rolls are good, when fresh, anyway."

Jackie had barely touched her roll. "I guess I should thank you for being there. You're good at this."

"I'm a thrill junkie. I jumped out of an airplane for my birthday a couple years ago, and discovered adrenaline. I signed up for the volunteer fire crew and became an EMT. The hours suck, but I feel like I'm doing more in the truck than in school."

"So you didn't always want to be an EMT?"

Roy shook his head. "I tried college for a couple years, dropped it, and got a real estate license. Second youngest employee in the company. Then—"

"Wait a second. Second youngest? How old are you?"

Roy smiled. "Twenty-five."

"Whoa. You look a lot younger."

"Yeah, I get that a lot. What about you?"

Jackie froze. "Uh. Hmm. Gee," She gave him a sidelong look. "Do you think you should ask me that?"

Roy shook his head. "I just wanted to make sure you were legal."

"Ha ha, very funny." Jackie frowned. "Are we continuing our speed date? This is hardly the time or place."

Roy smiled and looked her in the eye. Jackie felt a tingle that started at the back of her throat and shot down to her knees. Or maybe it was a pre-menopausal hot flash.

"You gotta admit, the atmosphere is lacking, but we can start where we left off. This is my turf, I haven't had dairy for three days, so I think you're safe."

Jackie couldn't help but laugh. "Okay. I'll jump. Let's just say my birthday is in March, and I used to be a teacher, until a kid pulled a knife six months ago."

"Je-sus," Roy muttered. "What happened?"

"He flunked. He's in juvie, and I'm in therapy." Jackie shrugged. "I have issues. Consider yourself warned."

Roy gaped. "But you're doing awesome. Really. Most people would be complete basket cases by now."

Jackie shook her head. "I'm worried about Trish. Focusing on someone else helps. When I 'settle down' I'll start having trouble breathing, get claustrophobic. Ergo, no driving. Crowded rooms are a problem, too. You think she'll be okay?"

It was Roy's turn to shrug. "I don't know. There's some internal bleeding, maybe a broken rib. She didn't tell you anything?"

"No. All I know is she had one of her dates tonight. She never mentioned his name, and had crossed him off her list, but then reconsidered." Jackie took a sip from her cup and realized it was empty. "I think she met him at that mixer."

"Damn." He crushed his coffee cup and got up, gathering used plates and napkins in quick, jerky motions. He stalked over to the garbage can and slammed the refuse on the lid, making it spin. "Don't they do a better screening job on those?"

"That's computer dating. This is totally different."

Roy gave a quizzical look. "Ah, you've done this before?"

Jackie smirked. "I tried online dating for a while. But my therapist wanted me to meet people face to face. She joined forces with Trish, and now here we are. Going gangbusters, don't you think?"

"Don't let what happened to Trish scare you. She'll say the same thing, when she's able." Roy's pager beeped. "Damn. Sorry, I've got another run." He paused, concern lining his features. "Will you be okay here by yourself?"

Jackie nodded. "I'll manage. I won't leave Trish."

Roy touched her shoulder. "Okay. I'll be back as quick as I can. She'll be fine, promise."

Jackie swallowed around the lump in her throat. She blinked rapidly and tried to smile. She put her hand over his. "Thanks."

He gave her shoulder a quick squeeze and left.

Jackie sat next to Trish's hospital bed, trying to ignore her bruises while they mocked daytime TV, when there was a knock at the door. A man entered and leaned against the door, holding roses. "Hey, Trish, I wanted to see how you're doing." Jackie saw Trish's hand move toward the call button.

"Hello, Mark. And goodbye Mark. Get in your precious Lexus and go away."

"Come on, Trish. I'm here with the olive branch. I just wanted to say how sorry I am."

Jackie was stunned. *This was Lexus guy? He was the one who beat Trish and threw her out of a moving car? And here he was. With flowers, for God's sake.*

"You heard her, Mark. You should leave."

Mark noticed Jackie for the first time. "This isn't any of your business, darlin'. Me and Trish are just going to work things out, try to start fresh. Why don't you leave us alone for a bit, hmm?"

At each syllable, Mark's voice faded. Instead, she heard the voice of the teenager who charged her in the classroom. When she told him he was repeating the grade, he pulled the knife. She hadn't fought back. She had cowered, terrified of a stupid punk, she realized.

Jackie stood and glanced at Trish, who had used the movement to grab the call button, and was pushing the button frantically. No help came. No nurse, no orderly, no one to check on her toilet paper.

Crap, it's just me this time.

Jackie sighed. "I've seen your type before. All 'Who me?' and 'aw shucks,' right? You really think you can hide behind that façade? I saw that crap in the classroom, and in my ex. You aren't fooling anyone."

Oh God, I don't know if I can do this.

"Now, look. I came to talk to Trish." Mark smiled. As he moved, sunlight from the window glinted off his Rolex, right into Jackie's eyes.

Just like it glinted off a knife in a classroom.

Just like it glinted off Dale's windshield, that last time. She didn't fight then, either.

Never again.

"You heard her. Get out."

Mark shook his head. "You don't get it. Trish and I are going to talk. Alone. She doesn't need your help. Get lost." He looked at Trish. "Call your friend off."

Jackie looked at Trish, who appeared tired and resigned. "Jacqueline, give us a few minutes. I'm fine."

Oh, shit, Trish.

Jackie screamed, grabbing the first thing in reach: Trish's cinnamon roll. She threw it, pelting Mark in the chest, leaving a dark smudge on his button down shirt.

"What the—" was all he got out before Jackie began throwing everything in reach.

"I told you," she shouted, throwing a small bowl of applesauce, "to get out," he ducked as a small plate sailed over his head, smashing into the wall, "of this room!" Jackie grabbed the orange juice and screamed again, splashing Mark with vitamin C and fiber.

Her screams and his shouts attracted the attention of nurses, a security guard, and EMTs within earshot, who all came running. *Oh sure, now you come*, Jackie thought.

Jackie pointed at Mark, panting. "He's the one who beat Trish!"

Mark put his hands up in protest. "This bitch is crazy! I came here to make peace, and she just attacked me. I didn't do a damn thing!" Mark wiped orange juice from his eyes.

The EMTs looked at each other and moved forward, grabbing Mark's arms. "Make peace, huh? For what, I wonder," one of them said.

"Hey, what are you doing?" Mark struggled against the men restraining him, whom Jackie recognized as Roy and his partner. During the scuffle, the rose bouquet Mark held dropped to the floor, unnoticed. Jackie relaxed a little and grasped Trish's hand.

The EMTs wrestled Mark toward the security officer, who handcuffed him and led him down the hallway. Roy and his partner stayed behind, looking at the food splashed around the room. Roy shook his head and whistled.

"Remind me not to piss you off until I've cleaned my plate. How'd you know Trish was in trouble?"

"She used my real name. That pisses me off more than being called Jake." Mark could still be heard yelling his innocence down the hall.

"Ah. Um, okay. Jackie, Trish, this is my partner, Scott."

Jackie released Trish's hand and moved to Roy. She pulled him to her, laying on the kiss she wanted to give him since their ride in the ambulance. Scott turned away, and Trish positively beamed through her bruises.

She let him up for air and held his shirt. "Okay, speed date, take two. I'm divorced, no kids, and a lousy housekeeper. I like sci-fi, sit coms, and action shows, Chinese food, and classic rock. I hate cats, and I have the full *Xena* collection, which I should pay more attention to, apparently. I have no idea if age will be an issue here."

"Wow," Roy breathed. "Um, okay. I'm a Wallflowers fan, single, and no kids that I know of, anyway. I'm convinced that pheromones know no age. I prefer Thai, and I wore the Autolycus costume at Comic-con.

Jackie smiled, leaning her head on Roy's chest.

"Sounds kinky," Trish said. "I have an idea. Get your own room, and get out of mine?"

Roy looked over Jackie's head. "Trish, Scott inherited his Porsche from his uncle, and I know where he lives in case he gives you any crap."

Scott looked puzzled. "This is speed dating? I thought you had to sign up or something." He waved at Trish. "'Sup?"

Jackie kissed Roy again. "Dinner, tonight, my place. Chinese, that's final. You can bring a Thai side dish, if you must. Skip the dairy."

Roy leaned over and picked up one of the fallen roses, handing it to her. "Done. Should I bring a Bruce Campbell movie?"

Jackie smiled, holding the rose to her face. It smelled wonderful.

"Let's watch it tomorrow morning."

Cyber Cupid

Linda Fisher

"Won't this man think he has a date with *you*?" Lily asked.

"Of course not," Amanda assured her. The two women sat at Starbucks waiting for the man Amanda had found online. Lily was so nervous they had showed up a half-hour early and Amanda didn't think she could handle another cappuccino. "After all, I used *your* profile on the Hot Men of Missouri dating site."

Lily's sister-in-law sat there looking a little smug. Amanda looked tall and lean in her tunic style turquoise top and black slacks, and with platform sandals she was nearly a foot taller than Lily.

"What did you do for a picture?" Lily was still fretting over what she referred to as a blind date.

"It was of you," Amanda assured her. "I scanned in that picture of you in Orlando."

"Good grief, Amanda, that picture was taken fifteen years ago."

"Don't worry about it. Everyone lies online. The guy you're meeting said he was thirty-two, so that means he's at least forty. He said he was six foot tall, so he's probably a short dude."

"I can't date a thirty-two-year-old! For heaven's sake, what were you thinking? I thought you put *my* info online, so how did this happen?"

"Dating a man five years younger than you isn't bad."

"I know I'm no math wizard, but thirty-one isn't five years younger than forty-seven. I never could subtract in my head, but even I can figure out that's closer to fifteen years than five."

"You are just being naïve. Everybody lies! I'm sure he doesn't look anything like his picture."

"You didn't tell me you had a picture. Show it to me."

"I don't have it with me, silly. It's on the library's computer."

"If you had told me he had a picture, I'd have looked at it. I don't need to spend all my library time looking for Christian romance books." Lily touched her hair, still surprised at how different she looked with the short, sophisticated style from Rhonda at the Mall Styling Salon. She loved the subtle brightening of her auburn hair. Her new Bare Minerals makeup had been applied with all the skill she learned during her makeover.

"Lily?" the young man stopped at their table.

"Yes," Lily said. "Do I know you?"

"I'm Brian," he said. He smiled at Amanda, "Are you Lily's mother?"

The color crept into Amanda's face. "No, I'm just her much older friend," Amanda said. "Lily, this must be the man you met online." She had created this monster and she wasn't about to give in to her temper now. She felt like giving him a Jethro Gibbs' slap on the back of his head.

Brian seemed oblivious to his faux pas and returned his attention to Lily "I recognized you immediately, Lily. You are even more beautiful in person than in your picture."

Translate that remark, Amanda thought, *as her breasts are much bigger. Amazing how much a breast enhancement ups the beauty scale.*

"How old are you, Brian?" Lily asked as she smoothed the full skirt of her sundress.

"Well, uh," he looked at his feet, "thirty-two?"

Amanda left the table to get a latte. She wasn't getting in the middle of this.

Lily pulled her specs out of her oversized genuine Coach knockoff and perched them on the end of her nose to get a closer look. "Brian, are you telling the truth?"

He glanced up at the board, "Could I get you something, Lily?" he asked.

"No thanks," she said. She didn't seem to notice Brian had evaded the question.

As Brian walked up to the counter to order, Amanda rejoined her at the table.

"He's so cute," Lily said.

"So are puppies," Amanda said, "but you don't date them."

"Don't be silly, Amanda. This isn't a date. It's just friends meeting for coffee."

"He isn't your friend, he's a stranger. You don't know anything about him."

"Sure I do, he's told me—I mean you—a lot about himself online, hasn't he?" Lily took a dainty sip of her Mocha Coconut Frappuccino. "Now hush so that he doesn't overhear you."

She smiled at Brian as he made his way back to the table.

"Would you like to go to a play at the Liberty Center?" he asked. "I have tickets for tonight's performance of *The Sound of Music*."

Lily glanced at Amanda who cocked an eyebrow.

"Oh, I love that show," Lily said.

Brian helped Lily arrange her new gauzy wrap around her shoulders.

"You kids don't be out too late," Amanda said.

Lily gave her a quick hug and whispered into Amanda's ear, "Thank you! You are a marvelous cupid!" As Amanda watched them walk away, she tried to drown her misgivings in her latte. *Just call me Cyber Cupid*, Amanda thought. *Like that was ever, in a million years, one of my goals in life.*

"I hope you enjoyed the show," Brian said as he crooked his arm through Lily's and walked her to the car. "How about Applebee's for dinner?"

"Oh, I couldn't possibly eat a meal," Lily said, "but dessert and coffee sound divine."

"Lily!" shouted a large woman with blue hair. She wore a sequined blouse that reflected a thousand points of light and a size small spandex pants stretched to the limit on a "one size fits most" derriere.

"Mrs. Bargmann," Lily said. Wasn't that the luck to run into the biggest gossip in town? She didn't offer to introduce Brian, because frankly, she did not know his last name. If Amanda had learned that information during the online exchanges, she hadn't shared that tidbit with Lily.

Not to be discouraged by a slight bit of rudeness, Mrs. Bargmann placed a hand on Lily's other arm in an overly friendly manner. "Aren't you going to introduce me to this handsome young man? He has to be Henry's son with those amazing green eyes."

Lily smiled sweetly ignoring the reference to her late ex-husband. "Dear Mrs. Bargmann, this is my date, Brian."

Mrs. Bargmann let go of Lily's arm and threw her hand over her mouth. The gesture was not for dramatic effect; the gossip diva was, for the first time in her life, speechless.

Lily and Brian walked away. Once they were safely out of the building, they giggled like two teenagers.

By the time they reached Applebee's, Lily had revised her order to a frozen strawberry margarita.

Over drinks, Lily learned that Brian lived in Warrensburg and taught creative writing at the college. Well, he didn't exactly say he was a professor, but that was what he implied. He seemed to know all about her. Apparently, Amanda had not been her normal taciturn self while pretending to be Lily.

After dinner, Brian drove up the long driveway to the farmhouse Lily and Amanda shared. He walked Lily to the door, and kissed her lightly on the forehead. "Would you like to do something next weekend?" he asked.

"Very much," she said. "See you then."

Lily closed the door and almost ran into Amanda in the dark.

"I think we've made a mistake," Amanda said.

"I don't," said Lily, "I really like Brian."

"Be reasonable. I'm not sure he's old enough to shave," said Amanda.

"He's thirty-two, and if he isn't shaving now, he never will," said Lily.

"You can't trust someone you know nothing about," said Amanda. "You don't want to wind up in barrel in Kansas like those poor girls who met that man online, do you?"

"You set this up, Amanda, so don't go back peddling now."

"He lied. He said he was thirty-two, which should have meant he was at least forty. Doesn't he understand the rules of online lying? Instead, he may be underage."

"I doubt that," Lily said.

"Why did his profile say he wanted a woman in her forties? You don't think he's looking for someone to adopt him, do you?"

"Brian's looking for someone mature. He's tired of immoral women. He wants a Christian woman who understands that love is more important than sex."

"Now, I'm really worried," Amanda said. "I'm going to have to check this guy out on Case.net. He must be some kind of a pervert."

"For crying out loud, Amanda. Why are you so negative about Brian?"

"This just isn't right. Why would a young man like that be sniffing around a woman your age? Use your head, Lily. You didn't tell him about your inheritance, did you?"

"Of course not! Money was the last thing on our minds," Lily said.

Lily piled her library books on the counter and headed back to the Christian romance section, while Amanda stopped to browse the newest suspense books. As soon as Lily disappeared behind the shelves, Amanda logged onto the computer. She pulled up Case.net and typed in Brian Silver. She wasn't sure why she hadn't thought to check him out before. Nothing popped up, but there was no proof that he had given her his legal name. The dating service was supposed to vet the members, but she knew that mostly consisted of filling out a survey.

Amanda glanced over her shoulder to make sure Lily was still out of sight, and she typed Brian's name in a Google search. His name filled the screen, and she selected one from a Warrensburg newspaper. Sure enough, Brian had used his real name based on the picture and the article.

"Oh, no," whispered Amanda. "What have I done?" She knew Lily was genuinely fond of Brian, and this article changed everything. How could she tell Lily? Should she tell Lily?

"Oh, there you are," said Lily from right behind Amanda.

Amanda wildly clicked the mouse to X out of the screen before Lily could see the picture. This was a delicate situation, and Amanda didn't want her to find out this way.

"Uh, yeah, I found books in the 'New' section and had some time to spare. Thought I'd just check Facebook."

"You are so clever, Amanda. Did you hear from Mary Beth?"

"Yes. She fixed lasagna for dinner last night." It was a safe bet that if Amanda had actually checked Facebook, her daughter would be talking about food. She loved to cook, especially Italian, and she had the girth to prove it.

Amanda and Lily sat on the porch drinking mint tea, watching the dust billow from behind Brian's SUV as he drove up the lane.

Amanda, for once, was in a dilemma as to what she should do with her knowledge. She had never been one to mince words, but this was a wrong she had done, and she wasn't sure how to correct it.

"Did you ever get him to fess up as to how old he is?" Amanda asked casually.

"Age doesn't matter," Lily said. "To his credit, he's never asked how old I am."

"Geeze, Lily, you are well preserved, but anyone can count the age spots on the backs of your hands and guess the decades as accurately as counting rings on a tree."

Lily glanced at her hands. They didn't look old to her, but then she wasn't wearing her glasses. She wasn't about to stretch her arms out to get a good look when Brian was climbing out of his Tahoe at that very moment. She fairly skipped off the porch, sundress swishing around her legs.

Brian kissed Lily on the cheek. He threw his arm around her shoulders and they chatted easily as they walked up the porch steps.

"Tea?" Lily asked.

"Looks great," Brian said.

What a cold-blooded cad, Amanda thought. *He isn't even sweating in this ungodly heat.*

They sipped their tea, and Lily showed Brian their flower garden. Amanda sat on the porch swing and stewed. She could hear Brian asking, "What is this plant?" and Lily supplying the answers. Amanda gritted her teeth and wondered if Brian's interest sounded half as phony to Lily as it did to her. Amanda was almost relieved when they moved farther away, and she couldn't overhear their conversation.

Amanda went inside to refill the tea pitcher. Lily slammed through the screen door and called out, "We're going to Warrensburg."

Amanda poked her head through the door. "What? Tell me that you aren't going to his house."

"Yes, and no. Not Brian's apartment, but to his home place. He wants me to meet his family!"

"He's taking you home to meet his mother? That sounds serious."

"I know," Lily grinned, "isn't it just too exciting? I'm meeting his dad and his sister—his mom passed away a few years ago."

Well, Amanda thought, *wonder how he's going to pull this one off?*

Amanda heard Brian's car pull up outside, and she pushed the curtain aside to get a better look. Lily jumped out of the car and ran up the sidewalk while Brian swung around the circle drive and headed back up the lane. "Well, I think there's been an awakening," Amanda said aloud. Brian had never failed to walk Lily to the door. Amanda flopped down into the La-Z-boy and switched on the TV.

"What happened?" Amanda turned off the TV when she saw Lily's tear-streaked face. "Wait. Before you tell me, I'll fix us a drink." She headed to the kitchen and Lily trailed along. Apparently, the story couldn't wait.

"It was awful," Lily said. "I was never so humiliated in all my born days. The 'sister' wasn't Brian's sister at all, she was his fiancée!" Lily dabbed at fresh tears with a dainty lace-trimmed hanky. Amanda had poured wine, but after Lily's announcement, she added more to each glass.

"Oh, my goodness!" Amanda said. Brian's engagement, and his real age—twenty-two—were the secrets she had been keeping from Lily. Now, she was kicking herself for not spilling the secrets.

"Was he after a *ménage a trios*?" Amanda asked.

Lily sniffed. "I don't know what that means, but if it means he's a low-down stinking turd, then that's what he was after."

"Oh. My. God," Amanda said. She gulped. "That freaking pervert!"

"He wasn't interested in me at all," Lily said. "He was just a, a, *fake*. When he introduced me to Brandi, his fiancée, he called me his much *older* friend. Emphasis on older! Older than what? Dirt?"

"He must have been interested in you if he wanted a threesome," Amanda said.

Lily gasped. "Threesome? Who said anything about that?"

"That's what a . . . oh, never mind, my mistake," Amanda said. "What was his point? Why woo you if he was already engaged?"

"He was looking for a woman for his *dad,* George," Lily wailed. "His bald-headed, paunchy stomached, opinionated, liberal democrat, old-hippy, pony-tailed dad! As if I would be interested in an old man like that!"

Amanda tried to hold back the chuckle. At first, her mirth was from relief. She covered her face and her shoulders heaved as she tried to control the laughter.

"Oh, Amanda, it wasn't *that* bad!" Lily rubbed Amanda's shoulders. "No need to cry about it."

Lily's sympathy was the final straw. Peals of laughter filled the kitchen until Amanda had to hold her sides. Lily began to laugh with her, although she wasn't sure why they were laughing.

Finally, Amanda, managed to say, "Brian's dad sounds an awful lot like my dearly departed husband."

"I knew he reminded me of someone!" Lily giggled.

"Oh, Lily, I'm so sorry I laughed. You had a traumatic experience, and instead of sympathy, I laughed about it."

"Well, that's okay. The reason I was so upset was because I thought you would be disappointed that your matchmaking was an abysmal failure."

"What? You were upset because of what I would think?"

"I didn't want to hurt your feelings, Amanda. You are my best friend in the entire world."

"I only want you to find someone, Lily. You seem so lonely. I'll never try to match-make again. I promise. I'm much too tall to be cupid."

Lily hugged her friend, and smiled. "You didn't do too bad, my friend." She pulled a slip of paper out of her purse. "George gave me his phone number and his email address."

"Email? You don't know how to use the computer," Amanda said.

"No, but you do! George would be perfect for you, Amanda!"

Lily's mouth turned up in a cupid's bow as she handed Amanda the slip of paper. Amanda hesitated for a moment, then reached out to take the offering. *The downside*, Amanda thought, *would be putting up with that worm Brian.*

AUTHOR BIOS

LISA RICARD CLARO is a freelance writer living in the Southeastern United States with her husband of thirty years. Lisa's articles and stories have been published in newspapers and online, as well as in *Writers' Journal* magazine and multiple anthologies, including *Chicken Soup for the Soul*. When not writing, she enjoys family time, visiting with friends, reading, and deciding what to write next.

For more of Lisa's writing, visit her blog, Writing in the Buff, at www.writinginthebuff.net. Contact Lisa at lisaricardclaro@bellsouth.net.

KATHRYN COIT experienced her first success in a writing contest at St. Fair Community College in the 1980s. Family and work responsibilities replaced time for creative writing efforts for many years, and her next success came with the opportunity to be published in the first *Shaker of Margaritas* last year. She and her husband Ben recently moved to Monterey, Virginia. They have one daughter, Erinne, two sons, Glen (recently licensed as a tattoo artist!), and Shaun. Her two lovely granddaughters, Ada and Helaina, are the light of her world! Kathryn is Regional Director and Case Manager for the Valley Program for Aging Services. This story is dedicated to her Camp Victory friends, especially to a roommate who lost her battle about a year later.

E. B. DAVIS writes mystery and romantic suspense. She blogs at http://writerswhokill.blogspot.com, and is a member of the Short Mystery Fiction Society, Sisters in Crime and its Chesapeake and Guppy subchapters. "Implicated by a Phrase" was published in *A Shaker of Margaritas: Hot Flash Mommas*, "Daddy's Little Girl" was published online at the website: http://voicesfromthegarage.com/story/daddys-little-girl and is the basis of her current work-in-progress novel, *Toasting Fear.*

In 2012, "The Runaway" will be published in the Guppy anthology, *Fishnets,* and "Lucky in Death" will appear in the

SinC Chesapeake Chapter's *Chesapeake Crimes: This Job is Murder,* a short story collection.

JENNIFER DICAMILLO is an award-winning writer, playwright, poet, and current President of Missouri Poets and Friends. She has won over 180 writing awards including an Honorable Mention from Writer's Digest, a CAPA nomination, a third place in an RWA contest, an Honorable Mention from *Byline Magazine*, and last, but not least, is an Eppie finalist. Her works have been featured in publications such as: *Grist, Turquoise Feathers, Museletter, The Poison Pen, Ozarks Monthly, Ultimate Horse Lovers Guide, Stride Magazine* (UK), *Storyteller Magazine* (US), *The Binnacle* (Univ. of Maine Press), *Taj Mahal Review* (Cyberwit, India), *True Confessions* (Dorchester), *Cup of Comfort for Women in Love,* and *Cup of Comfort for Cat Lovers* (Adams Media).

LINDA FISHER, Mozark Press, is the project leader and editor of *A Shaker of Margaritas: Hot Flash Mommas* and *Cougars on the Prowl.* She was editor and project leader of *Alzheimer's Anthology of Unconditional Love.* She has published three books of essays from her award-winning Early Onset Alzheimer's health blog. She has been published in *A Cup of Comfort, Chicken Soup for the Soul,* other anthologies, and online publications. Linda has won awards and prizes for her stories and essays. She is a member of the Missouri Writers' Guild, Ozarks Writers League, and the Columbia Chapter of the Missouri Writers' Guild. Her websites are www.lsfisher.com and www. MozarkPress.com.
She blogs at http://earlyonset.blogspot.com.

HARRIETT FORD is a three-time First Place award-winning author in both regional and national writer's contest. Her work appears in numerous short story collections, and she writes a humor/advice column for a weekly newspaper. She is the author of four books and is currently working on a Bible Study Guide

titled *If God Wants Me Well, Why Am I Sick*? Contact her at
www.deniedevidence.com

KARIN FRANK has written nearly her entire life. She
submitted her first story to her kindergarten teacher. No literary
review accepted it. After she graduated from UCLA with a B.A.
in Psychology, she worked for AT&T for twenty-five years.
After she retired from AT&T, she returned to writing. Her
poems have recently been published in the *Rockhurst Review*,
the *Taj Mahal Review,* the *I-70 Review*, the *Mid-America Poetry
Review*, and the *Coal City Review* as well as several other
magazines and anthologies. Poems have also been published in
several *Science Fiction* venues, her earliest love. *KC Voices*
recently published her first literary short story. She hopes to
publish many more.

MARCIA GAYE currently lives "a gentle life" in St. Charles,
Missouri. She enjoys writing in various styles of both fiction
and non-fiction, and has a memoir under construction. She has
lived in many areas of the United States, which broadens the
depth of her characters and settings. While evoking the
character of Janelle, she drew upon the rollercoaster emotions
of becoming single again in her mid-forties. She is now happily
married to a somewhat younger man, and reports that she counts
her blessings every day. Being a mother of two teachers
provides a sense of fulfillment and relief. Readers can find a
recent story honoring her maternal grandfather in *Cuiver River
Anthology V*. Mrs. Gaye is active in Saturday Writers, a chapter
of the Missouri Writers' Guild, and with Grace Church in
Maryland Heights, Missouri.

JANEL GRADOWSKI writes most often with her Golden
Retriever napping nearby. Her work has appeared in *Luna
Station Quarterly, Wired Ruby, Yellow Mama, Long Story
Short, Every Day Fiction* and several other publications. More
of her thoughts on many things can be found at her blog:
http://janelsjumble.blogspot.com.

CATHY C. HALL is a writer who makes her home in Georgia with her husband, plus Sally the Crazy Dog, and a couple of Junior Halls. She's published in both fiction and non-fiction, for adults as well as children. When she was in the eighth grade, she wrote a song to the tune of *Born Free* and her entire class sang it at graduation. She's liked big cats ever since.

TRACY HAUFF lives in the Rocky Mountains of Colorado and is an enrolled member of the Oglala Sioux Tribe. She has been published in magazines, trade journals, and in the online literary journal, *Stone's Throw Magazine*. She recently completed a novel, *Chokecherry: The Wild Story of a Bitter Young Woman*. An outspoken advocate for abused women and children, she has been an active volunteer for twenty-five years working with victims and survivors of abuse. She encourages everyone to visit her website, www.awomanofwords.com and her blog www.awomanofwords.typepad.com.

KATHY HOLMES often says that she was "Born in the City of Angels, raised on Walt Disney, and inspired by the dreams of both." She grew up halfway between Disneyland and the beach with influences from nearby Hollywood during the *Mad Men* era. No wonder there's usually some sort of retro scene in her writing. Tantalized by the tropics since Adam Troy set sail on the *Kon Tiki* in James A. Michener's *Adventures in Paradise*, Kathy has traveled to tropical destinations such as Hawaii, Florida, the Caribbean, Mexico, and Asia Pacific. Eventually, she moved to Florida where she wrote and secured representation for *Real Women Wear Red*, wrote for Walt Disney World and the *Orlando Sentinel*.

KIM LEHNHOFF is a Missouri wife, mother, stepmother, grandmother, and chocolate lover who is currently re-inventing herself as she waits for her next technical writing job to materialize. She has been published in the Mozark Press anthology *A Shaker of Margaritas: Hot Flash Mommas*. Kim is a member of the Writers' Society of Jefferson County and Saturday Writers in St. Peters, chapters of the Missouri Writers Guild. She enjoys spending time with family, blogging, reading, doing crossword puzzles, and has re-discovered her love of cooking and baking though she readily refers to herself as a Wilton cake decorating class dropout.

Kim blogs as June Freaking Cleaver at The Ratio of Failures, http://ratiooffailures.blogspot.com.

MARY ELLEN MARTIN has enjoyed writing her entire life, and writes in multiple genres. Her first published story was science fiction. She and her family call north Idaho home. She blogs at http://mehub.livejournal.com.

C.A.NEILSON has over twenty years experience working in the publishing industry as both writer and editor. She has written and published six books, one of which, *Miss Cornett's Courtship*, has been compared to a novella version of the best-selling *Cold Mountain*. Recent work includes a play *In His Service* based on the book *Celia, A Slave story*, a short film and feature screen play, *Once You Know*, based on a memoir about her historic bed and breakfast home. Before buying Romancing the Past Bed & Breakfast and relocating to Fulton, Missouri, she lived in Los Angeles, California, where she wrote and marketed several of her award-winning screenplays.

KATHY PAGE dabbles in many things, writing being one of them. She also enjoys participating in the local community theatre, reading, painting, and spending time with family and friends. Traveling is a particular enjoyment, which is good as she does quite a bit for both her paying job and volunteer work. She is on the national Board of Directors and an FDA Patient Representative for the Ekbom Disease Foundation. Kathy also does advocacy work for the American Cancer Society. Kathy enjoys an occasional challenge to keep life exciting.

DEBBIE PARKER lives in Columbia, Missouri. She has had both poetry and prose published in a variety of books and journals. Some of them include *Hot Flash Mommas*, *Notable Missouri Women*, and *Well Versed*. She teaches English to international students at Missouri University.

SYLVIA STRAUB turned to fiction writing following careers in academia and non-profit management. Mozark Press published her short story, "Dog's Best Friend," in its 2010 anthology, *A Shaker of Margaritas: Hot Flash Mommas*. She is currently working on a novel titled *Blood of the Shepherd*.

SUSAN ELIZABETH THOMAS lives in Moscow, Idaho, with her husband, Aaron, and their three children—Yesenia, Dakota and Novik. She loves to write, quilt, speak Spanish, and help out at her Southern Baptist Church and at various local charitable organizations. She is currently pursuing a master's degree in philosophy at the University of Idaho, and is president of an ACW writers' group, called *We Is Writers*. She has previously written for *Keys for Kids*, *The Secret Place,* and *Focus on the Family*. She was the first place winner for the Mozark Press *A Shaker of Margaritas: Hot Flash Mommas* short story competition.

SONIA TODD is a member of two writing groups, the ACW and the IWL. She has been previously published in *A Shaker of Margaritas: Hot Flash Mommas*, *Adventures in Mothering,* and the *Moscow-Pullman Daily News*. Sonia has been an invited speaker and writes a humor blog located at: http://myfirstlaunch.blogspot.com.

When she is not writing, Sonia can be found on Facebook at www.facebook.com/sonia.todd. She lives with her husband, two sons, and a dog named "Bunny" in Moscow, Idaho.

L. E. TOWNE has been writing fiction and poetry all her life, but has only recently become serious about it. A continual student of writing and the human condition, she uses her experiences to create believable characters in the drama called real life. Laura's work has been published in the *Midwest Literary Review* and *Mainstreet Rag*, her ten-minute play was selected for production in the Mendocino College play contest in 2008, and she was a finalist in the Emerging Writers Contest at the Southern Writers Symposium. She lives and works near Raleigh, North Carolina. Her latest story is "Don't Make Me Call the Flying Monkeys."

DONNA VOLKENANNT'S love for stories began as a child when her mother read to her *The Little Engine That Could*. Donna's reading tastes have changed since then, but she still favors stories with determined and inspiring characters who overcome challenges or great hardships. The real-life characters who inspire her are her husband and their two grandchildren, whom she and her husband have been raising since 2005.

When she's not reading, she's writing, revising, rewriting, reviewing, blogging, carpooling, or feeling guilty about the clutter in her house. She and her family, along with their black Lab Harley, live in the "Show Me" State of Missouri. Except for an occasional flood or a tornado, the Show Me State is a wonderful place to live, especially if you're a writer. Donna blogs at http://donnasbookpub.blogspot.com.

www.ingramcontent.com/pod-product-compliance
Lightning Source LLC
Chambersburg PA
CBHW061158170626
46809CB00003B/1148